"We have nothing more to say to each other."

"Emma!" Julien's fingers clasped her wrist when she turned to leave. "I am concerned for you."

"You have a strange way of showing your concern. Your friend Louis has not so much as laid a finger on me, while you make love to me one minute and ignore me the next." She blinked back her tears and raised angry eyes to his. "I feel used—cheap!"

"No, Emma, that is not so...." Quite suddenly he looked so dejected her anger melted away. "But I have no right to you, or any other woman, while I live with the shadow of a death I cannot account for."

What was he saying? Was he trying to make her see that he cared? Emma was more determined than ever now to discover the truth....

Books by Yvonne Whittal

These books may be available at your local bookseller.

Don't miss any of our special offers. Write to us at the following address for information on our newest releases.

Harlequin Reader Service
P.O. Box 52040, Phoenix, AZ 85072-2040
Canadian address: P.O. Box 2800, Postal Station A,
5170 Yonge St., Willowdale, Ont. M2N 6J3

YVONNE WHITTAL

cape of misfortune

Harlequin Books

TORONTO • NEW YORK • LONDON
AMSTERDAM • PARIS • SYDNEY • HAMBURG
STOCKHOLM • ATHENS • TOKYO • MILAN

Harlequin Presents first edition May 1985
ISBN 0-373-10790-0

Original hardcover edition published in 1984
by Mills & Boon Limited

CHAPTER ONE

'EMMA GILBERT, you're crazy! Do you know what you're doing? It took four years of hard work, not to mention the times you went without a decent meal to pay for your classes, to get where you are today, and now, after only two years in the teaching profession, you're throwing away everything you have achieved.'

Emma did not contradict her sister's statement. It had been prompted by a fierce anger and concern, and it had been the truth. With their parents dead there had been no money to back Emma, and she had worked almost day and night to pay for her studies. She could understand Lucy's bewilderment, for there had been times during the past weeks when she had doubted the wisdom of her own decision to resign her teaching post, but she had nevertheless gone through with it. She had kept this information to herself until after the Christmas holidays, but on this particular afternoon she could no longer hide the true facts from her sister.

'I need a change, Lucy,' Emma tried to explain while she cradled her mug of coffee in her hands and raised it to her lips.

'Why?' Lucy demanded, scouring a pan with unnecessary vigour and rinsing it before she placed it on the drying rack. 'You're a fantastic teacher, everyone says so, and it's what you've always wanted to be, so why this sudden desire for a change?'

'I feel as though I'm stagnating in my job, and there has to be more to life than attempting to teach a horde of ungrateful pupils.'

Lucy pulled out the plug in the sink and let the soapy

water drain away, and she wiped her hands on the kitchen towel before joining Emma at the table. She brushed a strand of fair hair away from her damp forehead, and her eyes were stern when they met Emma's. 'What you need, my girl, is a husband and children, and you can take my word for it that being a wife and a mother will keep you on your toes.'

A smile plucked at Emma's full, sensitive mouth. She could recall how Lucy, four years her senior, had drifted with ease into a marriage with Richard Bland. Lucy had always been a contented person, taking everything in her stride, and now, with two children as well as a husband to care for, she was obviously finding it difficult to understand why Emma could not have followed suit.

'When I meet the right man I'll consider settling down and having a family, but until then ...' Emma left her sentence unfinished, and Lucy snorted disparagingly.

'The trouble with you is you're too fussy,' she accused Emma. 'There have been plenty of nice men who would have suited you admirably, but you never once allowed any of them to get close to you.'

'Oh, Lucy,' Emma sighed impatiently, but she could not ignore the truth in her sister's accusation. She had never suffered a shortage of male companions over the years, but their amorous advances had left her cold, and each relationship had petered out as swiftly as it had started. She had not been able to tolerate the feel of their groping hands on her body and, when their hot mouths had sought hers, she had shuddered with something close to revulsion.

'What are you going to do now that you have given up teaching?' Lucy interrupted Emma's unpleasant thoughts.

'I'm still searching for something suitable.'

'Such as?'

Emma picked up the daily newspaper which was folded open at the Situations Vacant column, and she passed it to Lucy across the scrubbed wooden table. 'Take a look at that and tell me what you think of it.'

Lucy's glance slid quickly down the column until she found the advertisement Emma had circled with a red pen. *'Governess required for five-year-old child. Applicants must have the necessary qualifications.* Oh, *really!'* Lucy exclaimed angrily, breaking off in the middle of the advertisement to meet Emma's steady blue gaze. 'This is ridiculous! You would be nothing but a glorified servant.'

Emma rescued the newspaper from her sister's agitated hands and placed it on the floor beside her handbag. 'I have already applied and arranged for an interview. I have to see a *Madame* Perreau at the Wellington Hotel in two hours' time.'

'Madame Perreau?' Lucy jumped on the woman's name. 'Is she French, or something?'

'I think so, yes, judging from her accent on the telephone.'

Lucy's mouth tightened with disapproval, and she shook her head in something like disbelief when she met Emma's steady, almost defiant gaze. 'You're crazy!'

'You've said that before,' Emma reminded her humorously.

'And I'll say it again,' Lucy persisted. 'You're crazy!'

The Durban traffic was heavy, and the bus was delayed by the traffic lights, but Emma arrived at the Wellington Hotel with five minutes to spare, and was told to wait in the foyer until she was summoned to Madame Perreau's suite. Her appointment was for three o'clock, and while she waited she found herself recalling Lucy's last remark before she had left her earlier that afternoon.

'You're crazy,' Lucy had said, and Emma felt a smile tugging at the corners of her mouth, but it never quite materialised. Was she crazy? Was it ridiculous to give up everything she had worked for simply because she had felt she was getting nowhere and accomplishing nothing? It most probably did sound crazy to someone like Lucy who was placidly happy being simply a wife and a mother, but Emma felt neither placid, nor happy. She felt incredibly restless and driven towards something she could not explain even to herself.

'Miss Gilbert?'

Emma almost jumped at the sound of her name and looked up to see the uniformed desk clerk standing in front of her. 'Yes?'

'Madame Perreau will see you now,' he announced. 'She is on the ninth floor, suite number 903.'

'Thank you.'

Emma took the lift up to the ninth floor. If she had felt confident and calm before, then she felt nothing like that now, and her legs were unsteady beneath her when she stepped out of the lift and walked the short distance towards Madame Perreau's suite.

The door was opened mere seconds after Emma had knocked, and she found herself confronted by a slender, grey-haired woman dressed sombrely, but elegantly, in black, with a single string of cultured pearls about her throat to relieve the severity of her attire.

'Mademoiselle Gilbert?' the woman smiled, her pronunciation of Emma's surname giving it a pleasantly foreign sound.

'That's correct,' Emma replied, and she was ushered at once into the green and gold lounge.

'Please sit down,' the woman said in her heavily accented but perfect English and, when Emma had done so, she gestured towards the tray on the low table between their chairs. 'Do you take tea?'

'Yes, thank you, *madame*.'

Jewels sparkled on the fingers that held the teapot, and Emma watched in fascination at the elegance with which Madame Perreau performed such an ordinary task.

'Your tea,' she said moments later when she passed Emma her cup. 'Now we can talk.'

Emma felt as if it was expected of her to say something, but nothing came to mind as Madame Perreau's dark eyes surveyed her with interest, and something else which Emma could not define. It was a little unnerving, but she withstood this unusual scrutiny from the older woman.

'You are still young, *mademoiselle*,' Madame Perreau said almost accusingly, and Emma was instantly on the defensive.

'I'm twenty-five.'

The thin mouth smiled with something close to approval. 'You are a qualified teacher, am I correct?'

'Yes, *madame*,' Emma replied, passing her a brown, much handled envelope. 'You will find all my credentials in there.'

Madame Perreau studied the contents of the envelope while Emma sipped her tea nervously. She observed the older woman's features closely for some indication of her thoughts, but the lined face remained shuttered.

'You are fond of children?' Madame Perreau asked at length when she had returned the documents to the envelope.

'Yes, *madame*.'

'My grandson is five, and he will be attending school next year,' Madame Perreau explained after sipping daintily at her tea. 'I have cared for him these past two years, but I am not so young, and I can no longer cope. Also, my son feels that Dominic should improve his English, and I am not qualified to teach him.'

Where was the child's mother? The question hovered on Emma's lips, but instead she asked: 'Do you live here in Durban, *madame*?'

'No, *mademoiselle*.' Those thin lips curved into a smile once again. 'If you are found suitable for this post, then we shall require that you come to our home on the island of Mauritius.'

'Mauritius?' Emma echoed with a measure of surprise, but she wondered silently what Lucy would have to say about this unexpected disclosure.

'Living in Mauritius for a year does not appeal to you?'

'It appeals to me very much, *madame*,' Emma corrected hastily. 'I simply never imagined that the post you advertised would require living in Mauritius, and I was merely a little surprised.'

Madame Perreau nodded, obviously satisfied with Emma's reply. 'Do you have a passport, *mademoiselle*?'

'Yes, I do,' Emma assured her, and while they finished their tea she could not help thinking that this was the most unusual interview she had ever experienced, and she wondered if there had been many applications for this post. Did she stand a chance, or had she simply wasted her time in applying?

'*Mademoiselle*, it is my son who will decide whether you are suitable for the position,' Madame Perreau announced almost as if she had read Emma's thoughts. 'I wish you to leave this here with me.' A bejewelled hand tapped the envelope lying on the arm of her chair. 'And, if it is possible, I would like you to return again this evening at seven when my son will interview you personally.'

'I'll do that, *madame*, and thank you for the tea,' Emma answered politely as she rose to her feet, and moments later she was in the lift and being swept down into the foyer of the hotel. Did she dare hope that her application would be successful, or should she prepare herself for rejection?

Emma went home to her rented, furnished flat and tried not to think of the interview which still lay ahead of her. If she failed to acquire this post, then there would be others of an equally interesting nature, she told herself, but it did not stave off the restlessness which drove her into the kitchen to prepare a meal for which she had no appetite.

She dressed with more care that evening for her appointment with Madame Perreau's son, and she selected a blue silk frock which matched the colour of her eyes to perfection. Her golden brown hair hung straight to her shoulders, framing her delicate features, and giving her a young, vulnerable appearance which she would have given anything to disguise. Her wide, soft mouth curved in a distinctly mocking smile as she appraised herself in the mirror. She had always considered herself rather plain when she compared herself to her sister, Lucy, but it was not her physical attributes Emma was studying so intently. She was seeing beyond herself to the interview which lay ahead of her, and she was blind to the hidden, undiscovered secrets in the depths of her eyes. She was unaware, also, that men had been attracted by the tender promise of passion in the curve of her upper lip.

'You're crazy!' Lucy's remark flitted repeatedly through her mind, and an amused smile was still hovering about Emma's mouth when she finally stepped out into the warm January night and into the taxi which she had ordered to take her to the Wellington Hotel.

Stale cigarette smoke clung to the interior of the car and, wrinkling her nose, she turned down the window slightly as they sped along the well-lit streets of the city, but when she reached her destination she had an uncomfortable feeling that the odour of cigarettes had attached itself to her clothes.

The foyer of the Wellington Hotel was empty, except for a young man and a woman seated on a bench in the far corner, and they were so engrossed in each other that Emma felt certain they would not notice if the large potted palm beside them suddenly collapsed for some reason.

She announced the reason for her presence at the reception desk. The Indian clerk smiled his recognition, and she was told once again to wait. Being interviewed by Madame Perreau had not been much of an ordeal, but for some obscure reason Emma viewed her immediate future with infinite trepidation as she seated herself on the leather-bound chair and prepared herself to wait.

She was ten minutes early, and at precisely seven o'clock the desk clerk approached her, his footsteps silent on the thickly carpeted floor. 'Monsieur Perreau will see you now.'

'Thank you,' Emma murmured, her lips twitching into a nervous smile as she got to her feet and walked across the foyer towards the lift.

On the ninth floor she found herself knocking on Madame Perreau's door for the second time that day, and seconds later she was again confronted by that thin-lipped smile which now had a vaguely nervous appearance about it.

'*Bonsoir, mademoiselle*, and please come in,' she invited, and Emma stepped past her into the room with its concealed lighting. A man stood in front of the window with the curtains drawn aside to give him a view of the distant playground on the beach-front. His back was turned firmly towards them, and the very stillness of his stance drew Emma's attention, and held it. The superb cut of his black evening suit accentuated the leanness of his tall body, and his hair, so dark it was almost black, was worn short and trimmed neatly into his neck so that it only barely touched the stark white collar of his shirt. Emma heard the door close behind her, then Madame Perreau was saying in a quiet, almost reverent voice, 'Julien, this is Mademoiselle Gilbert.'

He turned then, one hand in the pocket of his jacket, and a slim cheroot dangling from the fingers of the other. Emma stared into those dark appraising eyes, and quite suddenly it felt as if someone had shut off the passage of air to her lungs by taking a stranglehold on her throat. She guessed his age somewhere between thirty-five and forty as she studied his lean features with the deeply tanned skin stretching tautly over high cheek bones and square chin. His heavy eyebrows were permanently arched in mockery above stabbing eyes, and beneath the acquiline nose the thinness of his mouth was relieved only by the faintly sensuous curve of his lower lip.

He was not good-looking by the usual standards, but he was certainly the most striking man she had ever met, and that aura of authority hovering about him simply added to his masculine appeal. Julien Perreau was not a man one could meet and forget the next instant. He was too vitally male for any woman to ignore, and Emma was suddenly aware of a frightened quivering in her breast.

Julien Perreau addressed his mother abruptly in French, obviously dismissing her, for she left the room quietly and closed the interleading door behind her.

'Do you speak French, *mademoiselle*?' he questioned Emma the moment they were alone, and the deep velvet of his voice did strange things to her quivering nerve-ends.

'No, *monsieur*,' she confessed, her mouth oddly stiff

and dry, and her mind vaguely registering the fact that her negative reply had not counted in her favour.

'After completing your studies you have been teaching for two years at a school for children whose ages range from thirteen to eighteen,' he voiced the information in the documents she had left in his mother's care.

'That is correct, *monsieur*.'

He drew hard on his cheroot and crushed the remainder into the marble ashtray on the table beside him, and his action conveyed a certain annoyance. 'What makes you think you are qualified to take care of a small boy who is only five years old?'

'I love children, *monsieur*, and children respond to affection no matter what their age.'

His mouth twisted cynically, but he did not comment on her reply as he gestured her into a chair and seated himself facing her. His English was perfect, she thought as she watched him light another cheroot and exhale the aromatic smoke through his nostrils. He spoke only with the slightest accent, and it added to the attractiveness of his deep, smooth voice.

'Why did you resign your post as a teacher?' he fired the next question at her, and his eyes were narrowed as he observed her through a screen of smoke.

'I felt the need for a change,' she replied truthfully, but quite suddenly it sounded like a lame excuse, and she had a horrible feeling that Julien Perreau thought so too when she glimpsed a hint of mockery in his shrewd, piercing eyes.

'You are running away from a man, perhaps, Mademoiselle Gilbert?'

'No, Monsieur Perreau,' she contradicted with a calmness she was far from experiencing. 'I simply felt the urgent need to do something different with my life.'

'English was not one of the subjects you gave tuition in.'

It was a statement, not a query, and she clasped her hands nervously in her lap, an action which did not go unnoticed as she said: 'No, *monsieur*, it was not.'

This was something else which did not count in her favour, but she sensed that there was more to come when he frowned down at the tip of his cheroot.

'What I had in mind for my son was someone older, *mademoiselle*; someone with experience of young children, and although you have the necessary qualifications to improve his English, you have not the practical knowledge to accompany it.'

He was telling her that she was unsuitable, not in so many words perhaps, but that was what he meant and, clutching her handbag, she rose to her feet with as much dignity as she could muster at that moment. 'I understand, *monsieur*, and I shan't waste more of your time, so——'

'Sit down.'

The quiet force of his words seemed to stun her, and she stared at him a little stupidly where he lounged in the chair facing her. 'I—I beg your pardon?'

'I said *sit down*. I have not yet dismissed you and, until I do, you shall remain seated,' he informed her autocratically and, much to her surprise, she found herself obeying him while he calmly knocked the ash from his cheroot into the ashtray at his elbow. 'I find you totally unsuitable, Mademoiselle Gilbert,' he continued to denounce her, 'but I no longer have the time to continue my search for a more suitable governess. I will employ you on a temporary basis, and after a trial period of a month I shall decide finally whether to continue employing you, or whether to search for someone more suitable.'

He mentioned a salary which was mind-boggling, and Emma's mouth almost dropped open in confusion and surprise. 'You mean you are offering me the job as governess to your son?'

'Do I express myself so badly, *mademoiselle*, or is it that you have difficulty in understanding?' he demanded derisively, and her cheeks went pink with embarrassment.

'You have made my unsuitability so clear, *monsieur*, that I—I am finding it difficult to believe that you actually want to risk employing me as a governess.'

Their glances clashed, awakening a flicker of antagonism, then he asked abruptly, 'How soon can you be ready to leave for Mauritius?'

'I shall need the weekend to pack,' she replied, a little shiver of excitement racing through her.

'Your passport is in order?'

'Yes, *monsieur*.'

'May I have your address?' he said, taking a small diary and a pen from the inside pocket of his dinner jacket and, when he had written down the address she had given him, he crushed his cheroot into the ashtray and got to his feet lithely to signify that the interview was at an end.

Emma followed his example, but the action brought her uncomfortably close to his lean frame and, despite her tallness, she found that she still had to crane her neck to look up at him. The woody scent of his masculine cologne mingled with the aroma of his cheroots, and together they formed a potent combination that stirred her senses in the most alarming manner. Never before had any man affected her in this way, and she was embarrassingly certain that Julien Perreau was well aware of her reaction to him. Annoyed with herself more than with him, she turned and walked towards the door, but that suave, faintly accented voice stopped her before she reached it.

'I shall make the necessary arrangements for your flight on Monday, and I shall see to it that the required documents for your stay in Mauritius are delivered to you in the morning.'

She turned to thank him, but the gleam of mockery in his eyes dried the words in her throat, and she left without uttering a sound.

'Well?' Lucy demanded when Emma telephoned her later that evening, and a multitude of questions were locked together in that one word.

'I've got the job,' Emma said, still finding it a little difficult to believe that she had been successful.

'Oh, lord!' Lucy groaned into Emma's ear.

'I'll be on trial for a month and, if I'm good enough, I'll stay on for the rest of the year.' Emma paused and bit her lip nervously. 'Are you sitting down?'

'Yes,' came the wary reply.

'Their home is on the island of Mauritius.'

The line was silent for a moment, then Lucy's voice demanded rather weakly, 'Emma, you're not really going to Mauritius, are you?'

'Why shouldn't I?' Emma laughed.

'But it's so far away, and we might not see you again for a whole year,' Lucy complained in a distinctly tearful voice.

'Oh, Lucy!'

The line went silent again, and Emma could imagine the struggle Lucy was having with herself before she asked calmly, 'When do you have to leave?'

'Monday.'

'So soon?' Lucy gasped. 'And what about your flat?'

'I'll have to pay a month's rental in lieu of notice.'

'Are we going to see you before you go?'

Emma bit her lip and mentally ticked off all the things which would have to be seen to before her departure. 'I'm not sure, I have so much packing to do, and——'

'Come over for Sunday lunch, then you won't have to waste time preparing something for yourself,' Lucy interrupted her eagerly, and Emma relented.

'That sounds like an excellent idea.'

They talked for a while longer, but it was only when Emma put down the receiver that she paused for the first time to consider what she had done.

She had accepted the position of governess to Julien Perreau's son, but that, in itself, did not present such a challenge. It was Monsieur Perreau himself who had presented her with the most difficult challenge of all. The physical impact of the man had disturbed her more than she would actually allow herself to believe, but the thought of living under the same roof with him was something she was beginning to dread. Even now her insides trembled at the mere thought of him, and she felt an uncommon tightness in her chest when her mind conjured up a vision of his lean, mocking features.

Emma thrust these disturbing thoughts from her mind and, realising that she had little time to waste, she took down her suitcases and sorted her personal things from those which belonged to the flat.

The Friday morning, as Julien Perreau had promised, the ticket for her flight to Mauritius and the necessary accompanying documents were delivered to her flat. Emma's hands shook when she studied them. It was reality, she was going to Mauritius, and if she did not hurry she would not be ready to leave early on the Monday morning.

Sunday lunch with Lucy and Richard at their Pinelands home was a welcome respite after two hectic days of rushing around. Their two little girls, Cathy and Wendy, aged four and two respectively, were excited about their Aunty Emma's visit, and Emma was happy to have them clambering all over her until Lucy put them to bed after lunch for their afternoon nap.

'What does this Julien Perreau do on Mauritius?' Lucy questioned Emma after returning to the dining-room and pouring their tea.

'I don't know,' Emma confessed frowningly.

'They grow sugar cane on Mauritius, don't they?' Richard chipped in, leaning back in his chair and patting the slight paunch he had developed since marrying Lucy. 'Perhaps he's a plantation owner.'

Emma pondered this suggestion for a moment, then she shook her head doubtfully. '*Plantation owner* is not a description that fits him very well. He's too ... too wordly, too aristocratic in his bearing, and too ... sauve, I guess.'

Richard's hazel eyes twinkled with mischief when they met Emma's. 'He must have made quite an impression.'

'Will you be living in the same house with him?' Lucy butted in before Emma could think of a suitable reply to cover up her confusion.

'I presume so.'

'I don't think I like that very much,' Lucy frowned worriedly, 'but I suppose his wife will be there to keep it all respectable.'

'I don't think he has a wife.'

'*What?*' Lucy cried, almost choking on her tea.

'I said I don't think he——'

'I heard what you said,' Lucy interrupted Emma sharply. 'Where is his wife, then?'

'I don't know.' Emma felt that odd tightness in her chest again. 'Neither Monsieur Perreau, nor his mother mentioned the existence of a wife.'

'Perhaps he's divorced,' Richard suggested helpfully, but Emma could not imagine that any woman in her right mind would look at another man when she had someone like Julien Perreau.

She was vaguely shocked at her own thoughts, but it

was time to leave, and Richard very kindly offered to drive her back to her flat.

'Emma ... you will be careful, won't you?' Lucy demanded anxiously.

'Give the girls a kiss for me when they wake up, and stop worrying,' Emma laughed forcibly, and she hugged Lucy for the last time. 'I'll write to you and I'll give you all the details as soon as I know more about the Perreau family.'

Lucy did not look wholly satisfied, but there was no time to say more. Richard had started up the car and, knowing how impatient he could be, Emma hurriedly got in beside him.

'Lucy is very worried about you,' Richard stated the obvious when they drove away from his home. 'I don't think she will rest until you're safely married to someone respectable.'

'I know,' Emma sighed. 'It's her prime concern to marry me off to someone, and it has become the proverbial thorn in my side.'

'Don't you want to get married?'

'Not at the moment,' Emma replied, becoming bored with the conversation, and wishing suddenly that Richard and Lucy would stop pestering her in this way. 'I'm quite happy as I am.'

'I wouldn't wait too long, if I were you. You're not getting any younger, you know, and once you're set in your ways you might as well forget about marriage. You won't want to give up your independence for a man, and you'll end up on the shelf.'

Richard had spoken in jest, but Emma felt annoyance pulsing through her veins, and she chose to remain silent rather than start an unnecessary argument with someone she was really quite fond of.

He said 'goodbye' to her eventually with a hug and a brotherly peck on the cheek, and she felt vaguely uneasy when she entered her flat and stared at the two suitcases which stood packed and ready for her departure in the morning. On the floor in her bedroom stood an open suitcase into which she had to pack the last minute things, and in her handbag was her ticket for the flight to Mauritius.

Their conversation at the luncheon table had disturbed Emma. What did she really know about the man she was going to work for? He had a mother who was charming, but obviously a little wary of him, and he had a five-year-old son named Dominic. For the task of taking care of his child and improving his English, she had been offered a salary which was far beyond anything she had ever expected, but other than that she knew nothing about the man in whose home she would be living.

Several questions raced through her mind for which she did not have an answer. The one that troubled her most was: Where was his wife? And why had neither he, nor his mother mentioned her? Surely his wife had some say in the personal and academic education of her child?

It was really none of her business, Emma finally decided, and with that thought in mind she resumed her packing.

CHAPTER TWO

THE Boeing was preparing for take-off. Emma leaned back in her window seat and closed her eyes. She was quivering with excitement and a certain amount of trepidation, but when she felt the giant aeroplane lifting its nose into the air, there was only one thought in her mind that stood out above all the others. *It was too late to change her mind.* She had given up a safe and secure job for something in which there would be no security at all. She had no idea what the future had in store for her, and she knew even less about the people and the country she was going to live in.

The No Smoking sign went off, and everyone began to relax. The burly, grey-haired man seated beside Emma lit a cigarette and opened his briefcase. He was obviously used to flying, and looked quite bored with the whole idea, but it was still a comparatively new experience for Emma. Refreshments were served as the silver-winged Boeing left the South African coastline behind it and flew eastward across the Indian ocean. When the stewardess paused beside them Emma chose tea, but the man beside her preferred a whisky.

Emma took out the informative little book on Mauritius which she had bought at the airport and, when her empty tea cup had been removed, she studied it closely. Her companion, his tongue loosened after a second whisky, closed his briefcase with a decisive snap, and turned slightly in his seat to face her.

'Is this your first trip to Mauritius?' he asked, gesturing towards the book she was reading.

'I'm afraid it shows, doesn't it,' she could not help

laughing, but only someone who knew her well would have heard that quiver of nervousness in her voice.

'I go there on business four or five times a year, and although the magic of the island never diminishes, I find the flight a tiresome necessity,' her companion informed her with a rueful smile. 'I presume you're going on a holiday?'

'I'm afraid not,' she contradicted his assumption. 'I've taken the position of governess to Julien Perreau's small son.'

'Julien Perreau?' the man repeated, a slight frown between his bushy eyebrows.

'Do you know him?' she asked, her heart thumping nervously.

'I know *of* him.' He lit another cigarette and took his time explaining. 'Julien Perreau is a very wealthy man, if one can believe the locals. He owns one of the largest sugar plantations on the island, and he is also the owner of an hotel he had built at Tamarin some years ago. Other than that I have been told that he has a financial interest in various businesses on the island. I don't know very much about his private life, I'm afraid, but there was talk two years ago that his wife died under tragic and rather mysterious circumstances.'

So he is a widower, the thought leapt into her mind. She felt inexplicably relieved, but her eyes were clouded with concern and curiosity when she glanced at her companion. 'What do you mean by *tragic* and *mysterious*?'

'Well,' he began reluctantly, shrugging his heavy shoulders, '*Tragic* because his wife apparently fell down the steps of his home and broke her neck in the process, and *mysterious* because no one seems to know, or want to talk about how and why the incident occurred.'

There was something decidedly sinister about his disclosure, but there was compassion in her voice when she murmured, 'How terrible it must have been for him.'

'No doubt you will learn more about it once you're working for him.'

Emma did not reply to this, but learning about the strange circumstances in which Julien Perreau's wife had died left her feeling vaguely uneasy, and considerably troubled. Was there something sinister about the way his wife had met her death, Emma wondered, or was she simply allowing herself to be frightened for no reason at all?

The man beside her opened his briefcase once more, and Emma returned her attention to the book on Mauritius which she still clutched in her hands, but her concentration had descended to zero. She was reading, but she was taking in nothing at all, and she finally relinquished the effort to allow her mind to wander at will.

If Julien Perreau's wife had died under tragic circumstances, then she could understand that he did not wish to discuss it with anyone, and that, she imagined, could evoke sinister speculations. It was unfair, really, but it was a natural reaction, she decided, her logical mind assimilating the information she had received. To jump to a hasty conclusion would be wrong, and most especially since she had no knowledge of Julien Perreau as a person. She was curious, though, but it was not in in her nature to pry and, unless someone saw fit to enlighten her, she would not ask.

The Indian ocean sparkled far beneath her in the morning sunlight, and it stretched as far as the eye could see, its colour ranging from deep blue to turquoise in places. Emma channelled her thoughts in a different direction, and tried to imagine what Mauritius would look like. The travel booklet described it as a tropical island with crystal clear, coral-protected sea gently washing the white sand, and there were pictures of giant palms silhouetted against the crimson sky at sunset. It looked idyllic, but the reality was seldom what the travelogues led one to believe.

Lunch was served on the plane, and they were told to advance their watches three hours to the Mauritian summer time. Emma was too excited to eat, and her tray was removed almost untouched. Soon she would have her first glimpse of the island of Mauritius and, despite her wariness of the future, she looked forward to setting foot on Mauritian soil.

The No Smoking sign flashed on above Emma, and moments later the air hostess' voice announced: 'We have begun our descent to Plaisance International Airport. Please make sure your seat is in the upright position, fasten your seat belts, and extinguish your cigaretttes. Thank you.'

Emma snapped her seat belt shut and leaned towards the window as far as she could. She could see the coral reef and part of the coastline in the distance. They were approaching the island swiftly, and her heart was beating in her throat. The Boeing dipped lower, and the white sandy beaches made way for a landscape of rivers winding their way in and out among the mountains, and sugar cane fields. Villages nestled on hillsides and in basins, and Emma wondered what lay ahead of her as the Boeing dipped lower towards the south-eastern part of the island where the airport was situated.

They landed at four-thirty Mauritian time that afternoon, and Emma was grateful to get out of the shimmering heat on the tarmac and into the cool airport building. She had to wait to collect her luggage, and it took time to get through customs. With her suitcases piled on a trolley, she glanced around at her fellow passengers and, when she noticed the creased state of their clothes, she was pleased that she had chosen a floral silk dress in which to travel.

'Will someone call for you, or could I offer you a lift?'

Emma turned to face the burly man who had sat beside her during the flight, and she smiled reassuringly. 'I'm expecting someone to meet me.'

He nodded abruptly and, wishing her a pleasant stay, he walked away. Five minutes later she wondered whether she had not perhaps been a little optimistic. Her eyes scanned the people lounging about in the airport building, but there was no sign of a familiar face.

'Mademoiselle Gilbert?' a voice enquired and she turned sharply to face a man of Chinese origin who was dressed in blue, open-necked shirt and shorts.

'That's correct,' she replied hastily when the query deepened in his dark, almond-shaped eyes.

'My name is Li Ho Kee,' he introduced himself, bowing politely in true eastern style.

'Monsieur Perreau sent you to meet me?'

'Oui, mademoiselle.' Unsmiling, he stepped towards the trolley laden with her suitcases. 'Follow me, s'il vous plaît.'

Emma followed him towards the exit, her eyes on his sandalled feet, and a nervous knot at the pit of her stomach. There was also a vague disappointment spiralling through her at not being met by Julien Perreau, but she knew it was ridiculous to feel that way. Why should he make an effort to meet *her*, an employee, when he could simply send someone to collect her?

A silver Bentley stood parked at the entrance, and Emma's eyes widened when Li Ho Kee unlocked the boot and deposited her suitcases into it. The rear door was opened for her, and seconds later they were speeding away from the airport.

They travelled northwards along the coast, passing two fishing ports before going inland towards Pamplemousses. The flame trees were in full bloom, their flame red flowers brilliant in the shimmering afternoon sunlight, and wherever she looked the bougainvillaea and oleanders added an extra dash of colour to this exotic island. It was a tropical paradise, the travelogue had been correct about that, but her curiosity as to her destination could no longer be suppressed.

'Where are we going?' she asked the silent man in the driver's seat.

'To the villa of Monsieur Perreau at Cap Malheureux,' came the abrupt reply and, sensing that the Chinese chauffeur had no desire to indulge in an enlightening conversation, Emma lapsed into silence once more.

Cap Malheureux. Cape of misfortune, Emma translated the name for herself and, from what she had read, this had been an unpredictable part of the coast where vessels had often come to grief.

They travelled between the sugar cane plantations where long-skirted Indian women tilled the soil. The road twisted, dipped and rose again as they drove north-east towards the coast. Li Ho Kee was an expert, if somewhat arrogant driver, and the islanders leapt hastily for the side of the road when the Bentley sped along the narrow laned villages where lava-stoned walls surrounded holiday cottages and villas.

The sign posts indicated that Cap Malheureux was but a short distance away, and Emma's heart began to beat a little faster. They were driving along the coast again, and she caught repeated glimpses of an attractive stretch of sand and coral sea. Palm trees stood tall and proud against the clear blue sky, and beyond the reef a lonely wind surfer glided swiftly southwards along the coast.

Cap Malheureux lay directly ahead, and bungalows nestled among the trees, but Emma was quite suddenly overcome with nervousness when the Bentley nosed its way between stone pillars to begin a slight descent towards a sturdy, but attractively built two-storeyed house. Bougainvillaea, in its various shades, trailed profusely along walls and across pergolas, while flame trees and poinsettias added a more vivid splash of colour in the vast grounds surrounding Julien Perreau's home. The windows were not shuttered on this glorious day as the Bentley slid to a halt beneath the flight of stone steps leading up to the patio with its colourful awnings above the entrance and the windows which faced the ocean.

The Chinese chauffeur opened the door for Emma to alight, and she stepped stiffly out on to the paved driveway at the exact moment when Madame Perreau made her appearance at the top of the flight of steps. She stood there, proud and dignified in her bearing as she watched Emma ascend the steps, and only when Emma stood beside her did a faint smile touch her thin lips.

'Welcome to Ile Maurice, *mademoiselle*, and welcome also to my son's villa.' She extended both hands to clasp Emma's briefly. 'You have had a pleasant flight?'

'Very pleasant, thank you, *madame*,' Emma replied politely.

'Li, take Mademoiselle Gilbert's luggage to her suite,' Madame Perreau instructed the man who had followed Emma up the steps with two of her three suitcases, then she turned her attention to Emma once more. 'Come, *mademoiselle*, I have ordered tea to be brought to the *salon*, and afterwards I think there will be sufficient time for you to freshen up before dinner this evening.'

The villa was cool inside as Emma followed Madame Perreau into the spacious entrance hall with its attractive black and white tiled floor. An impressive staircase led to the upper floor, but Emma felt her breath catch in her throat when they entered the *salon*. The enormous room was a fantasy in cream, gold, and emerald green. The décor was modern, but with a touch of the old, and to Emma it was as if she were looking at a picture in a glossy magazine. It was every woman's dream to possess a home such as this, but Madame Perreau looked vaguely ill at ease in these picturesque surroundings when she gestured Emma into a chair and proceeded to pour tea into delicate china teacups.

'When do I meet your grandsom, *madame*?' Emma broke the somewhat strained silence after she had taken a sip of her strong, sweetened tea.

'Dominic is being taken care of by the servants,' the older woman smiled almost apologetically. 'You shall meet him tomorrow.'

They drank their tea in silence, and Emma expected at any moment to see Julien Perreau's dynamic presence gracing the *salon*, but he did not put in an appearance.

'You have a lovely home, *madame*,' Emma remarked, placing her empty teacup on the table beside her chair and rising to her feet to wander across to the window which overlooked the garden.

'My home is in Roches Noires. I have been living here at the villa with my son since . . .' Madame Perreau paused, a flash of guilt in her dark eyes when Emma turned to glance enquiringly at her, then she continued hastily, 'For two years I have been living here.'

So, Madame Perreau had moved into the villa after the death of her daughter-in-law, Emma discovered, but her calm features gave nothing away when she turned again to glance out of the window.

Her eyes eagerly scanned the colourful view from the *salon*. 'The garden is beautiful, and in particular the roses.'

'Julien has Li to thank for that,' Madame Perreau replied, a hint of warmth returning to her voice. 'Li takes care of the garden and, when it is necessary, he is also the chauffeur.'

Emma's mind was full of queries when she turned from the window, but she dared not question Madame Perreau who was busy rising to her feet.

'Come, I will show you up to your suite,' she said, and Emma followed her from the *salon*, across the hall, and up the carpeted stairs with the curved iron balustrade.

Three passages led out from the landing on the second floor, but Madame Perreau turned towards the right and pushed open a door at the end of the passage. She gestured Emma to precede her into the room, and yet again Emma felt her breath catch in her throat. The small, private lounge was furnished with padded, biscuit-coloured chairs to match the shaggy carpet, and the drapes at the window were a deep, cool blue. The décor in the bedroom beyond was the same, but the furniture was modern and painted white, with the slatted doors of the built-in cupboard and dressing table adding an attractive finish.

'Oh, *madame*, this is beautiful,' Emma exclaimed delightedly, feeling more like a guest than an employee.

'I hope you will be very happy here,' Madame Perreau smiled stiffly. 'Do not trouble yourself with the unpacking. I will send someone up later to attend to it for you.'

Emma wanted to protest that this was not necessary, but Madame Perreau had taken her leave so abruptly that there had been no opportunity to say anything. She stared at her suitcases standing neatly at the foot of the bed with its blue satin cover, and had to admit to herself that she was in no mood yet to unpack. The thought of someone doing this chore for her was an unaccustomed luxury and, after a moment of deliberation, she decided she would take advantage of this service. What she needed most at that precise moment was a wash and a change of clothing, but, before she could do more than wash her hands and sponge her face, there was a knock on the door of her suite.

'*Monsieur* wishes to see you,' the young Indian girl announced when Emma had opened the door. 'I will show you the way.'

Emma's heart missed an uncomfortable beat at this summons, and she hastily brushed her hair and applied a little make-up before following the girl from her suite.

Downstairs in the mirrored hall they turned in the opposite direction to the *salon*, and the young girl knocked lightly on a panelled door before she opened it. She announced Emma in French, and the next moment that deep, velvety voice replied, '*Merci*, Nada.'

The girl stood aside and gestured Emma into the room, and when Emma stepped forward she found herself in a spacious study with sliding glass doors leading out on to the patio at the entrance of the house.

'*Bonjour, mademoiselle,*' Julien Perreau welcomed her as he rose from behind the carved, wooden desk, and his height alone was sufficient to intimidate her. 'I hope you had a pleasant flight?'

'Yes, thank you, *monsieur.*'

His dark eyes flicked over her in an impersonal manner, but it was enough to make her feel embarrassingly sure that he had taken in every detail of her appearance, and plenty more besides.

'There are one or two matters I wish to discuss with you, if you would please sit down.' He gestured with a well-shaped hand towards the chair on the opposite side of his desk, and he waited until she was seated before he also sat down. The top buttons of his white silk shirt had been left undone to expose his sun-browned throat, and the play of muscles beneath the expensive material made her realise that he had looked deceptively lean the last time they had met. 'As from tomorrow Dominic will be in your care,' he informed her rather brusquely. 'I shall leave it entirely up to you how, when, and where you decide to give him tuition in English, but I shall expect results. Dominic has his meals in the dining-room, but his dinners in the evenings are sent up to his room at six so that he may go to bed early. I shall, however, expect you to dine with my mother and myself at seven-thirty each evening.'

Emma swallowed nervously. 'Yes, *monsieur*.'

'You are free on Wednesday afternoons from two to six to do as you please, and if you need an evening free it can be arranged that my mother, or one of the servants will take care of Dominic.'

'Thank you, *monsieur*.'

'If there is anything else you wish to know, then my mother will gladly assist you.' He rose behind his desk, indicating that the discussion was at an end, and Emma hastily followed suit. 'Dinner is at seven-thirty, do not forget, and here on Mauritius the dress is casual, unless it is a special occasion.'

'Thank you, *monsieur*,' she said again.

'You may go,' he dismissed her, and when she turned towards the door she was alarmed to discover that her legs were shaking.

Julien Perreau was really the most unusual man she had ever met, she decided when she made her way upstairs to her suite. He made her feel nervous and afraid, and she could not imagine why. He was a man like any other, she tried to tell herself, and there was certainly something about him that appealed to her as a woman, but his cold, unsmiling features had come close to making her feel that he despised her. Did he despise her in particular, or did he despise women in general? It was a puzzling thought, and she could not imagine why it had leapt into her mind, but she was not going to let it spoil her stay on this lovely island.

Her clothes had been unpacked, and the suitcases had been removed from her room during the short period she had been out of her suite. Her personal toiletries had been placed on the dressing table and, when she glanced at her wrist watch, she found that she had almost an hour at her disposal before dinner. Emma chose to spend it in a relaxing bath, and when she finally emerged from the bathroom she selected to wear a cool cotton frock which left her creamy shoulders bare except for the thin straps. She applied her make-up with more care than when she had been summoned so unexpectedly to Julien Perreau's study, and the sun had set on her first day on the island when she eventually went downstairs.

Lights, like teardrops against the walls, lit her way down into the hall. A magnificent crystal chandelier hung from the high ceiling, and its light was reflected in the carefully placed mirrors against the walls. Contrary to what she had imagined, Emma had no difficulty in finding the dining-room, for Julien Perreau and his mother were having, what sounded like, a heated argument. They were speaking rapidly in French, and Emma simply followed the sound of their raised voices until she found herself in the dining-room with its panelled walls and marble-topped furniture.

They were standing beside a glass cabinet when Emma entered, and their argument ceased abruptly the moment they became aware of her presence. The tension in the atmosphere was like a waft of chilling air blowing up against Emma and, while Madame Perreau's features still registered a disapproval which was directed at her son, Julien Perreau's face remained cold and expressionless. Emma felt as if she ought to apologise for intruding, but the gleam of mockery that leapt into Julien Perreau's eyes told her that he was not only fully aware of her uncertainty, but also interested to see how she was going to react. Detestable man!

'I suggest we sit down to dinner,' he announced abruptly when Emma made no move to advance or retreat from the room, and when they were seated at the table he rang the silver bell which had been placed conveniently close at hand.

Julien Perreau filled their glasses with Burgundy wine while they waited for their consommé to be served, but the wine did not ease that strange tension around the dinner table, and no one, least of all Emma, seemed inclined to want to enter into any sort of discussion.

Vindaya was served as a second course, and Madame Perreau relaxed sufficiently to explain that it was a Creole speciality. 'It is fried fish which has been marinated in spices, garlic and vinegar.'

It tasted absolutely delicious, but it was followed by yet another spicy dish which consisted of pork served with a Chinese sauce and fresh vegetables. A fruit dessert and coffee concluded the most exotic meal Emma had ever eaten, but she might have enjoyed her first Mauritian meal a great deal more had she not been so aware of the autocratic man seated at the head of the table.

Emma went directly up to her room after dinner, but it was such a beautiful night that she ventured downstairs again after a few minutes, and strolled out on to the darkened patio at the entrance of the house. The warm night air was scented and free of the tension which had lingered throughout dinner, and Emma breathed the air deeply into her lungs. She wondered what Julien Perreau and his mother had been arguing about, but then she told herself it was none of her business, and contented herself instead with the peaceful night sounds around her.

Across the moonlit sea lay a wedge-shaped island, and it protruded from the water like the crest of a mountain which had at some time disappeared into the ocean. It was, like Mauritius, a volcanic island, and she sighed with the pure, unadulterated pleasure of finding herself in such exotic surroundings.

'You find the view impressive?'

At the sound of that velvety voice her breath almost locked in her throat, and she pivoted nervously to see Julien Perreau's tall, shadowy figure leaning against the low concerete wall and a little distance from her. He was smoking a cheroot, she could smell the aromatic tobacco now as it drifted towards her and, for some inexplicable reason, she felt herself begin to tremble.

'You have a beautiful view of the sea from your villa,' she heard herself answering calmly.

'You have been here to Mauritius before?'

'No, *monsieur*,' she managed without a tremor in her voice when he lessened the distance between them until she could see his striking features clearly etched in the moonlight. 'This is the first time.'

'You will no doubt want to see something of the island on your free afternoons?'

'I hope to do that, *monsieur*.' Did she detect a hint of mockery in his query, or was it her imagination.

'You may start your sightseeing right here this evening.' He stepped behind her and pointed over her shoulder towards the sea. 'That island you see there is the *Coin de Mire*, or Gunners' Quoin. It is named so because it is shaped like the wooden wedge used under a cannon.'

He was standing so close to her that she could feel the heat of his body against her back, and an odd, but pleasurable little shiver rippled through her. 'How far is the island from here?'

'About four kilometres.' He moved away then, and

she felt strangely bereft. 'Mauritius itself is only sixty-one kilometres long, and forty-seven kilometres wide, and it is entirely of volcanic origin.'

Julien Perreau leaned against the wall close to her and, although she could not be sure, she felt certain that those dark eyes were observing her intently. It made her feel uneasy, and her mind searched frantically for something to say which would break the silence between them.

'How long have you lived here on the island, *monsieur*?' she finally asked the first question that leapt into her mind.

'I have lived here all my life,' he informed her, and she sensed, rather than saw, the mockery on his shadowed features.

'And yet you still speak French in your home?' she pressed on.

'I speak French in my home, and Creole to my fellow islanders.' He drew hard on his cheroot until the tip glowed red in the darkness, then he flicked it over the wall into the garden. 'English is our official language here in Mauritius. It is taught in the schools, and it is used very much in business.'

'I see,' she murmured, and at that precise moment the telephone rang shrilly in his study.

'*Excusez-moi, mademoiselle*, I have been expecting this call.' He pushed himself away from the wall and turned towards the sliding glass doors, but he paused there to say an abrupt, '*Bonne nuit.*'

'Goodnight, *monsieur*,' she responded, but when he had gone she lingered out on the patio a few seconds longer to enjoy the cool breeze which drifted up from the direction of the sea.

The telephone stopped ringing and Julien Perreau's voice filtered quite clearly out on to the quiet patio. 'Daniella, *chérie*.'

He was speaking to a woman, that much Emma understood, but the conversation was conducted in a rapid burst of French. She felt as if she were eavesdropping despite the fact that she could not understand what was being said, and she entered the house quickly to go up to her room, but in the hall she encountered Madame Perreau. Her son's voice was muted through the panelled door, but every word could be heard quite clearly, and the older woman's face registered once again that grim disapproval Emma had noticed when she had entered the dining-room earlier that evening.

'You are going up to bed?' she asked, making no effort to hide the fact that she had been listening in on the conversation behind that panelled door.

'Yes, *madame*,' Emma replied, feeling decidedly uncomfortable. 'Goodnight.'

'*Bonne nuit, mademoiselle.*'

The older woman's features did not lose their grimness, and Emma was more disturbed than she wanted to admit even to herself when she hastily climbed the stairs up to her room. She was beginning to suspect that Madame Perreau's disapproval had something to do with the woman who had telephoned, and it was also quite possible that Julien Perreau's telephone conversation could relate directly to the argument he had had with his mother before dinner that evening.

'It's none of your business!' Emma rebuked herself fiercely, but an hour later, when she lay sleepless on her bed in the darkened room, she was still wondering about the strangely tense situation here at the villa.

The villa was situated in such beautiful surroundings that its inhabitants ought to be extremely happy, but Emma was beginning to suspect that there was very little happiness in this house. It was as if a sombre

shadow had settled over the house, affecting everyone
who lived in and around it, and Emma shivered
involuntarily when she allowed her mind to wander.
Her travelling companion's expression had sobered
instantly at the mention of Julien Perreau's name, and
Li Ho Kee had been sullen and uncommunicative when
he had collected her at the airport. Madame Perreau
had made a definite effort to smile when she had
welcomed Emma on her arrival, but the Indian girl,
Nada, had been rigid-faced when she had summoned
Emma down to Julien Perreau's study, and the nearest
Julien Perreau had come to smiling had been when his
mouth curved with derision and mockery.

Why? Could the circumstances of his wife's death
have something to do with it, or was his association
with this Daniella woman responsible for the unhappy
situation in the villa?

Unable to sleep, Emma slipped out of bed and
walked barefoot across the room to the open window.
It was an exquisite night, the stars were like diamond
clusters in the sky, and the perfume emanating from the
roses seemed to hang heavy in the air. It was a night for
lovers to go walking on the beach in the moonlight, but
the villa was devoid of love, or lovers.

A movement caught her eye down on the patio, and
she drew a careful breath when she saw Julien Perreau
pacing about with that now familiar cheroot dangling
from his fingers. He looked troubled and also a little
lonely. It seemed as if he was fighting a private battle,
and Emma felt a strange compassion tugging at her
heart. She knew an impulsive desire to join him down
there on the patio, to share his troubled thoughts, and
to comfort him if necessary.

She drew back from the window, startled by the
feelings racing through her, and her body was trembling
so much that she had to lean against the wall for a

moment to steady herself. What on earth was the matter with her? It was absolutely crazy to want to offer comfort to a man she barely knew, and common sense warned that any attempt to do such a ridiculous thing would merely evoke his mockery.

She heard him mutter something like a curse, and there was such a ring of anguish to it that it felt as if someone had stabbed a knife into her soul. This autocratic man was human after all, and the discovery did something to her which she dared not pause to analyse. It frightened her as nothing had ever succeeded in doing before, and something warned her that she was fast becoming the prey of the serpent in this lovely paradise.

CHAPTER THREE

THE sun rose early on Mauritius, but Emma had been up before dawn. Her first night at the villa had been a restless one, and she wondered what this day would have in store for her. The most important person of all she had not met yet, and she was feeling extraordinarily nervous about it. What if the child took an instant dislike to her? This negative thought constituted failure before she had even begun, and she thrust it aside, quite determined not to fail.

Dressed in a cool lemon-coloured frock and rope sandals, she brushed her hair with an unnecessary vigour. Her skin was flawless, but she applied a little make-up and, when she put down her lipstick to examine the result, there was a knock on the door to her private lounge.

'Coffee, *mademoiselle*,' Nada announced when Emma opened the door, and she carried the tray across the room to the low table beside the window where Emma had drawn the curtains aside earlier that morning.

'Thank you, Nada,' she smiled, admiring the girl's long, glossy black hair which was combed away from her face to hang in a neat plait down her back.

Nada acknowledged her thanks with a brief nod of her head, but there was no answering smile on her lips, and her dark eyes were downcast when she walked out of the room and closed the door quietly behind her. Emma's smile was replaced by a frown, then she shrugged off the Indian girl's rigid soberness, and poured herself a cup of coffee.

The dew lay heavy on the grass in the garden, and the

scent of the roses drifted up to her window to fill the room with their fragrance. Emma leaned back in her chair while she drank her coffee, and she savoured the silence which was disturbed only by the birdsong in the trees. She was not by nature prone to bouts of anxiety, but her nerves had been set on edge by an undercurrent of tension here in the villa which she could not understand. It was possible that she was allowing her imagination to get the better of her, but that did not explain this feeling deep down inside of her that something was seriously wrong here in the Perreau home.

She placed the empty cup on the tray, and leaned back in her chair once again to make a few mental plans for the day ahead of her, but she found it difficult to do so without knowing the child who had been placed in her charge. Dominic Perreau was a stranger to her, and it was possible that her ready-made plans might go awry. It would be safer to play it by ear on her first day at the villa, and to build up a daily routine from there.

Emma could not be sure how long she sat there pondering this question, but something, a sound perhaps, made her turn her head to see a small boy standing in the open doorway, and he was observing her with an intense speculation in his tawny eyes. This had to be Julien Perreau's son. There was a strong resemblance in the colour of the boy's hair, and there were definite signs that the child had inherited his father's acquiline nose and square jaw. His mouth was small, however, and although it was pursed she could see that one day it would be fuller than his father's.

'Hello?' Her smile projected a natural warmth, but she had a curious sensation that, if she rose to her feet, he might be frightened away. 'You must be Dominic.'

His wide, speculative glance did not waver, but he ventured farther into the room. '*Oui*, I am Dominic.'

'My name is Emma,' she responded, sitting forward in her chair, but making no visible attempt to persuade him to come closer to her. 'Do you speak English?' she prompted when he simply stood there staring at her.

'A little,' he replied, his eyes wavering for the first time.

'Do you want to learn to speak English properly?'

'*Non.*' His eyes clouded and his mouth drooped at the corners. 'But *Papa* say I must.'

'I can't speak French, and I would very much like to learn.' His sullenness vanished almost as swiftly as it had appeared, and Emma adopted a slightly con-spiratorial air when she asked: 'If I teach you to speak English properly, will you teach me to speak French?'

Emma knew that she had succeeded in crossing the first and most important hurdle when a smile quivered about his mouth, but Dominic confirmed it by stepping right up to her chair and saying with childish enthusiasm, '*Oui, mademoiselle.*'

She felt like hugging him, but common sense warned that it was too soon for such a demonstrative act. She glanced at her wristwatch instead, and she was surprised to discover that an hour had passed since Nada had brought her a tray of coffee.

'Is it time to go down to breakfast?' she asked, rising to her feet and, when Dominic nodded, she held out her hand with a forced casualness. 'Let's go, then.'

Dominic hesitated only a moment, then his warm little hand slipped into hers, and they went downstairs together.

Breakfast was served beneath the shade of the bougainvillaea on the east-facing terrace of the villa. It overlooked part of the rose garden, but the flame trees and poinsettias were predominant with their scarlet flowers accentuated against the green backdrop of the ebony trees. Julien Perreau and his mother were seated at the white, wrought-iron table, and Emma's heart skipped an uncomfortable beat when her stern-faced employer looked up from his newspaper at their approach.

'*Bonjour, Papa,*' Dominic greeted his father in a stangely hushed voice, and he remained stoically at Emma's side even though she had released his hand.

'*Bonjour, Dominic ... mademoiselle.*' His cold, impersonal eyes skimmed over her. 'I see you have already met Dominic.'

'Yes, *monsieur*,' Emma heard herself replying in almost the same hushed tone Dominic had used, then she turned towards the woman seated at the other end of the circular table. 'Good-morning, *madame.*'

'Good-morning, *mademoiselle.*' Her features remained rigid, but there was a definite softening in her eyes when the child walked up to her and kissed her on the cheek. '*Bonjour*, Dominic, and I hope you are going to eat your breakfast this morning?'

'*Oui, Grandmère,*' he answered in that subdued manner which Emma found puzzling, but this was not the time to wonder about such things, and she shrugged it off mentally.

Emma sat down facing Dominic, and she poured out a glass of fresh orange juice for both of them. She seldom ate breakfast, but she was tempted by the fresh rolls, cold ham, and cheese, and she helped herself while Nada served Dominic with a nutritious cereal.

'If our continental breakfast does not appeal to you, then Nada will prepare bacon and eggs for you,' Julien Perreau announced from behind the morning newspaper, and Emma looked up from buttering her roll to meet his glacial glance.

Was he trying to find fault with her, or was he merely

being polite? She could not decide, and her voice was cool when she said: 'Thank you, *monsieur*, but this is quite sufficient.'

He knew he had annoyed her, that sudden gleam of mockery in his eyes told her so, and it unnerved her to discover that this man seemed to have the uncanny knack of reading her thoughts. She would have to be more careful in future, she warned herself, and she was immensely relieved a few minutes later when he rose from the table and announced that he was driving down to Tamarin.

Julien Perreau looked deceptively lean in his beige suit and white, open-necked shirt, but Emma suspected that his body was muscled and in peak physical condition. Her eyes followed his tall frame unobtrusively when he entered the house, and a few minutes later the Bentley sped past with her employer at the wheel.

Madame Perreau sighed softly, but Emma heard her and, glancing at Dominic, she noticed that he, too, appeared to be more relaxed. Her own nerves appeared to be uncoiling themselves slowly, and she was once again left to wonder at the effect Julien Perreau seemed to have on his entire household.

The telephone rang somewhere in the house, and moments later Nada stepped out on to the terrace.

'Telephone for you, Madame Celestine,' she announced, then she added something in rapid French.

'Excuse me, *mademoiselle*,' the older woman said apologetically as she rose from the table. 'I am having the hot water system repaired in my home at Roches Noires, and they appear to be having problems.'

Emma murmured something appropriate and, left alone at the table with Dominic, they finished their breakfast in silence.

'Let's go for a walk in the garden,' Emma said eventually, pushing back her chair and rising to her feet.

Dominic expressed neither enthusiasm nor resentment at her suggestion, but he silently accompanied her down the shallow steps into the garden, and he gradually began to thaw sufficiently to point out the places where he enjoyed playing. A wooden shelter was one of these places, and Emma could imagine why. It was cool inside, and shaded and protected by the roses which ranked so profusely along its walls and across the thatched roof. They sat down next to each other on the rough wooden bench, and after a while Dominic pointed straight ahead of them.

'The sea, *mademoiselle*,' he said, his eyes staring wistfully at the crystal clear water lapping the sandy shore.

'How lovely to have the beach practically on one's doorstep,' Emma sighed, then she shifted her glance from the sea to study the little boy beside her. He was much too serious and subdued for a child of his age, but circumstances had obviously moulded him into this severe behaviour pattern. 'Do you swim, Dominic?'

'*Non, mademoiselle,*' he shook his head, and that wistful expression deepened in his eyes.

'Dominic . . .' She placed her hand lightly on his T-shirt clad shoulder, and he turned his head sharply to look at her with a hint of anxiety on his face that touched her heart in a way nothing had ever done before. She had wanted to make the offer to teach him to swim, but instinct warned her not to make rash promises without consulting his father, and she said instead: 'Please call me Emma.'

'Emma,' he repeated slowly, then he added in his hesitant, heavily accented voice, 'It is . . . pretty.'

Pretty? It was the last word Emma would have chosen to describe her name, but Dominic's lack of a more appropriate adjective filled her once again with that impulsive desire to hug him. She suppressed it swiftly, however, and merely smiled at him.

'I'm glad you like it,' she said, but she was still of the opinion that her name was so plain it was almost ugly.

Children respond to love no matter what their age, she recalled her own words of but a few days ago, and Dominic responded now with a shy smile that tugged rather painfully at her heart.

He took her along the path that led to the beach, and once they were on the sand they took off their shoes to wade ankle deep in the water. They walked for some distance along the shore, but the heat of the sun finally drove them back to the villa, and they arrived in time to have tea on the terrace with his grandmother. Afterwards Emma took Dominic up to her lounge for his first English lesson.

She had bought a few books before her departure from Durban, but she had to improvise considerably to accommodate Dominic's age, and she found that Dominic, despite his initial announcement that he had no desire to learn English, was a clever and intelligent pupil. He was too small to settle down to serious studies and, guided by her knowledge of her nieces, she somehow succeeded in making a game of these lessons in English to which Dominic responded with an enthusiasm she found rewarding. He was also very subtle for his age. He had taken her at her word and, half way through the lesson, she discovered that he was reversing their rôles from time to time. It amused her at first, but her genuine desire to learn French prevailed, and she found herself repeating the French words and phrases as dutifully as Dominic repeated them in English.

The chair at the head of the dining-room table was conspicuously empty when they went down to lunch, and Emma found herself glancing at it repeatedly. 'Doesn't Monsieur Perreau come home for lunch?'

'Not always,' Celestine replied, her hand touching the glass bowl beside her plate. 'Can I pass you the salad, *mademoiselle*?'

'Thank you,' Emma replied hastily, taking the bowl and helping herself to the spicy tomato and lettuce salad, then she glanced at the woman seated close to her. '*Madame* ... it would make me feel very much more at home if you would call me Emma.'

Madame Perreau's dark eyes met Emma's, and for one brief moment Emma thought that her friendly overture was going to be rejected, then the woman's thin lips softened into a smile that actually put a touch of warmth into her eyes.

'I would like that ... Emma,' she said slowly, and Emma felt her own rigid features relaxing into a smile which radiated a warmth of which she was unaware.

It was customary in the Perreau household to rest for at least an hour after lunch, Emma discovered, and she welcomed the idea. It had been a long morning, and there had been moments of tension which had sapped her energy along with the hot, humid climate on the island.

Dominic's room was two doors down from her own. It was spacious, and the furniture was of solid pine. It was a boy's room, with cinnamon-coloured drapes at the window, and a large assortment of aeroplanes and cars set out neatly on the shelves beside the built-in dresser. He had his own private bathroom, and everything else a boy could wish for, she realised as she pulled back the cover on his bed and took off his sandals, but, when she looked up into his solemn face, she knew without doubt that he lacked the most important thing of all. *Love!* His grandmother adored him, that much was obvious, but it seemed as if Celestine Perreau was afraid to show it, and his father ...! Emma pulled her thoughts up sharply. She was delving too deeply into circumstances which did not concern her, and she knew also that she would have to guard against becoming too attached to Julien Perreau's son.

Emma went to her own room and, taking off her dress and her sandals, she stretched out on the bed. The room was cool, and she might have slept if her mind had not been so restless in its pursuit for understanding. What was the reason for the tension which prevailed at the villa? Julien Perreau's wife had died two years ago, long enough for any man to overcome his sorrow at losing a wife. Surely they were not all still living under the shadow of her death? She shivered at the thought and made a deliberate attempt to shut her mind to the mystery surrounding the Perreau family. She thought of Lucy and Richard instead, and decided that she would write to her sister when she had time to herself after dinner that evening.

Dominic wanted to go down to the beach again that afternoon after tea, and Emma did not object to taking him. They walked in the shallow water and played on the sand, and on two occasions Emma actually succeeded in making him laugh. On the first occasion the sound of his laughter was so incredibly wonderful that she sat back on her heels and stared at him, but almost instantly he adopted an embarrassed air as if laughter was something to be ashamed of. The second time was when she had squealed with fright at narrowly missing putting her bare foot on a small crab which had emerged from beneath a rock, but this time Emma had laughed almost as much as Dominic at her own silliness, and their shared laughter forged a bond between them that very afternoon.

At bath time that evening Dominic proved that he was quite adept at managing on his own, and he was in his pyjamas and gown when, promptly at six, Nada brought his dinner in on a tray and set it out on a small table beneath the window.

'Don't you say thank you?' Emma gently reprimanded Dominic when he accepted this service in silence.

'*Merci*, Nada,' he responded at once, and Emma saw Nada smile faintly for the first time.

Celestine Perreau came in a little while later to say 'goodnight' to Dominic, but she did not linger while he finished his meal.

'I suppose your *Papa* will be coming up soon to say goodnight to you,' Emma remarked conversationally while she put him to bed.

'*Non,*' Dominic replied, snuggling down between the sheets.

'Doesn't he ever come and tuck you in?' she questioned, carefully hiding her surprise and, when Dominic seemed at a loss for words, she prompted, 'Sometimes?'

'Sometimes,' he repeated, his eyes clouding. '*Papa* is very busy.'

A spark of anger rose within Emma at the thought of Julien Perreau treating his son so coldly, but she decided not to judge him too hastily. Perhaps pressure of work *did* prevent him from spending more time with Dominic, and it would be unkind of her to condemn him outright.

'Well, I'd better get myself ready for dinner, or I'll be late,' she smiled, glancing at her watch, then she brushed her fingers lightly through his dark hair. 'Goodnight, Dominic, and sleep well.'

'*Bonne nuit*, Emma,' he smiled, and his smile remained with her throughout the silent dinner she shared with Julien Perreau and his mother.

Alone in her room later that evening, she wrote a long letter to Lucy, but she carefully avoided mentioning the incidents which had disturbed her since her arrival. Lucy would worry, Emma knew that, and she decided that her sister had more than enough to cope with without still having to worry about someone else.

'You're crazy!' Lucy's accusation leapt unbidden into her mind, and Emma put down her pen with a sigh. She may well have been crazy to accept this position in the Perreau home, but she was here now, and she would see it through to the end.

On her first afternoon off Emma went shopping in Curepipe. Li and the Bentley were at her disposal, Madame Perreau had informed her, and Emma did not quibble. To find some other mode of conveyance would have been difficult at that stage, and neither did she want to insult the Perreaus by refusing their generous offer of the use of their chauffeur driven car. It was awkward, but she resigned herself to it temporarily.

Curepipe was the centre of a sizeable tea industry, and the town was larger than Emma had imagined it would be. It was a hot afternoon with rain clouds shifting purposefully across the sky, and it was during her tour of the shops when she discovered that the locals jokingly spoke of their town as having only two seasons: the rainy season, and the season of rains.

Emma left the colourful shops behind her and, with time to spare before meeting Li at the parking area close to the Royal College, she decided to explore the town. She wanted to see as much of Mauritius as was humanly possible during her free afternoons, and it was almost as if she had been led into the botanical gardens which were known for their nandia palms which grew in the water. In these tranquil and attractive surroundings she could shake off the little incidents which had troubled her at the villa, and time lost its meaning for her in this peaceful oasis. Why was there no peace and tranquillity at the villa? The setting was right for it, but instead the atmosphere in and around the villa was vibrant with tension. Why? She would have loved to continue her stroll through the gardens while she pondered this question, but when she glanced at her watch she knew that it was time to leave in order to meet Li at the appointed place.

It was raining when Li drove Emma back to Cap Malheureux, but it was so humid that her skin felt hot and clammy when they finally arrived at the villa. She thanked Li and went straight up to her room with her parcels to bath and change into something cooler and, when she entered the dining-room at seven-thirty, she found only Celestine Perreau standing at the window staring out into the darkness beyond.

'*Madame?*' Emma questioned, her concern aroused when she saw the grim, almost disapproving expression on the older woman's face. 'Is there something the matter?'

'Dinner will be a little late this evening,' she announced without turning. 'Julien telephoned a little earlier to tell me that he will be bringing Daniella Bertrand with him this evening.'

'Oh,' Emma breathed, recalling her first evening at the villa when she had heard Julien Perreau answer his telephone and speak the name 'Daniella'.

'Daniella lectures in science at the Royal College in Curepipe,' Madame Perreau explained, turning away from the window and gesturing agitatedly. 'She is a very clever woman, and she is very beautiful, but she has no heart. Sometimes I think they deserve each other, but I also know that what my son needs is a warm and loving wife to melt the ice around his heart.' She paused abruptly, and there was an apology as well as despair in the way she spread out her hands. 'I do not know why I am telling you this.'

Emma smiled and gripped Celestine's hands in a spontaneous attempt to comfort her. 'You have taken me into your confidence, *madame*, and I shall not repeat what you have told me.'

'Yes, I trust you, I can feel it, and *le bon Dieu* knows there are days I do not even trust myself,' Celestine sighed with the merest hint of a smile on her lips as her cool fingers tightened about Emma's, but the next instant she withdrew her hands nervously. 'I think I hear Julien's car.'

The atmosphere was suddenly tense, and it spiralled higher when Julien Perreau entered the dining-room with Daniella Bertrand's slender hand resting in the crook of his arm. Madame Perreau made no pretence of how she felt about her son's association with this slender, dark-haired beauty and, after the introductions were made, the meal progressed in a strained silence which was broken only by the *sotto-voce* conversation between Emma's employer and the slow-eyed woman seated on his left. They spoke in French, making it impossible for Emma to understand more than a few words here and there, but she finally began to suspect that it had something to do with a scientific discovery which could benefit the sugar industry. The words *sucre* and *scientifique* cropped up all too frequently to be missed and, while Daniella Bertrand did most of the talking, Julien Perreau listened attentively.

'You are a teacher, *mademoiselle*?' Daniella addressed Emma unexpectedly in English when the dessert had been served, and Emma felt vaguely uncomfortable with everyone's attention suddenly focused on herself.

'Yes, I am.'

'What are your subjects?' Daniella delved a little deeper into the subject with a speculative and assessing gleam in her dark eyes.

'I taught history and biology.'

'You did not teach English?' Daniella demanded, making it sound almost like an accusation, and Emma felt her back stiffen.

'English was one of the subjects I studied, but I majored in history and biology,' she explained.

Daniella Bertrand put down her spoon and adopted a haughty attitude. 'How, then, can you expect to teach Julien's son English?'

'Mademoiselle Gilbert is on trial for a month, Daniella,' Julien Perreau intervened almost as if it was a *fait accompli* that she would not last longer than a month, then his cold, expressionless eyes shifted from Emma to the woman whose classic features now wore an outraged look.

'But how inconvenient, *mon cher*, if you are forced to find a replacement,' Daniella protested, her hand touching his arm with an easy familiarity which Emma somehow found disturbing and discomfiting.

'There will be no need to find a replacement,' Celestine Perreau intervened sharply as if she found the thought distasteful. 'Emma will manage very well in improving Dominic's English.'

Julien Perreau's eyebrows rose a fraction at Celestine's intervention. 'Let us hope you are right, *Maman*, and that . . . Emma does succeed.'

He had paused briefly before the use of Emma's name to glance at her, and the icy mockery in his eyes had made her shiver inwardly.

Coffee was served during the ensuing silence, and when Emma finally risked raising her glance, she encountered a warmth in Madame Perreau's eyes which banished some of the chill in her veins.

Emma excused herself from the table a few minutes later, and went up to her suite. She prepared a lesson for the following day, and afterwards settled down with a book she had bought in Curepipe, but her mind was

not on what she was reading. Her thoughts drifted back
to her first evening at the villa, and the argument she
had witnessed between Julien Perreau and his mother.
She knew now that her initial assumption had been
correct; Madame Perreau did not approve of Julien's
association with Daniella Bertrand, and Emma now
understood the grim disapproval on the older
woman's face that evening when she had encountered
her in the hall. Celestine had been eavesdropping on the
conversation between her son and the woman she
obviously despised, and she had made no attempt to
hide what she had been doing.

The situation at the villa was becoming more deeply
disturbing with every passing day, and when Emma
finally went to bed she found herself wondering whether
she would always succeed in remaining aloof from the
incidents which created such a tense atmosphere in this
lovely home.

During the weeks that followed Emma settled down
comfortably into a routine which was both pleasurable
and educational for Dominic as well as herself. The
child was learning rapidly, and very gradually he was
developing into a normal, happy boy, but in his father's
presence he was still the subdued child she had
encountered on her arrival. There were many things she
could not fathom in this odd relationship between
father and son, and there were many things about it
which annoyed her so greatly that she often had to bite
her tongue not to speak out.

Emma spent one of her free afternoons swimming
and sunbathing on the beach. It was a relaxing treat she
had promised herself since her arrival, but somehow
there had never been time for it. On this particular
afternoon, however, she had indulged herself. After a
quick swim she took care to use a lotion on her body to
screen her from the stinging rays of the Mauritian sun.

She spread out her beach towel on the incredibly white sand and made herself comfortable and, with the sun beating down on her body, she actually succeeded in shutting her mind to all the things which had annoyed her lately.

She lingered too long on the quiet stretch of beach in her reluctance to return to the reality she would have to face at the villa, and it was close on six o'clock when she hurried up the path towards the villa. Seeing a strange car parked in the driveway made her hesitate momentarily, then she quickened her step. She did not want to have to face strangers at this precise moment, but a strange male voice brought her to an abrupt halt when she stepped on to the patio.

'Ah, what have we here?' he drawled, his English heavily accented, and Emma turned to find herself confronted by Julien Perreau and a man who was not quite as tall, but equally dark.

His bold eyes swept her from her tangled hair down to her sandalled feet, taking in her slimness beneath the short towelling robe, and lingering deliberately on her smooth shapely legs, but his bold appraisal did not disturb her as much as Julien Perreau's brief, impersonal glance.

'This is Mademoiselle Emma Gilbert,' Julien introduced her tersely. 'She is Dominic's governess.'

'*Bonjour*, Emma,' the stranger used her name glibly and without her permission. 'I am Louis Villet, an old friend of Julien's, and it is no wonder he has kept you hidden here at the villa.'

A brief, uncomfortable silence followed during which she glimpsed the hardening of Julien Perreau's lean jaw and, painfully aware of the way she looked, she said hastily, 'If you will excuse me I must go up and change.'

'I hope we meet again, Mademoiselle Emma,' Louis

Villet remarked as she turned towards the entrance of the house. 'In fact, I am sure that we shall meet again.'

She glanced at him briefly over her shoulder, but she did not bother to answer him, and she was in such a hurry to get away that she was actually out of breath when she reached her room.

Louis Villet's manner had been boldly sexual, but it had left her untouched except for a rising irritation. Julien Perreau's cold glance had shaken her more. It had left her feeling naked, and embarrassment sent a new wave of heat into her cheeks that made her rush into the shower as if to wash away the memory of it.

At the dinner table that evening Emma could not look at her employer, and she was inordinately relieved that Louis Villet had not been invited to join them. No one spoke during the meal, which was not unusual, and Emma excused herself as soon as she could to retire to her room.

She tried to shake off the incident on the patio by settling down with a book, but an hour later, when there was a knock on her door, she realised that she had simply turned the pages without taking in a single word.

She got up to open the door with her book still clutched in her hand, and her heart leapt into her throat when she found Julien Perreau standing there. His light grey suit accentuated the darkness of his hair and the deepness of his tan, but it was his eyes that caught and held her attention. They were narrowed and searchingly intent as if he were seeking for something, but she had no idea what.

'May I come in?' he asked eventually, and she had been so unnerved that it took an effort to pull herself together.

'Yes, of course,' she replied hastily, standing aside and opening the door wider.

He walked past her, and that aura of authority which

clung to him made her feel as insignificant as a little grey fieldmouse. She invited him to sit down, but he declined politely, and Emma felt obliged to remain standing on legs which were not as steady as she would have wished.

'You have been here a month, *mademoiselle*, and *Maman* informs me that Dominic's English has improved remarkably.' It angered her to know that he had not taken the trouble to find out for himself, but had had to rely on his mother's observations with regard to his son's education, and she had great difficulty in biting back the words that rose to her lips. 'You will be happy to stay on until the end of the year?' he questioned, giving her the feeling that he could not care less whether she went, or stayed.

'I have grown fond of Dominic, *monsieur*, and I would like to stay,' she answered simply.

'Then we have an agreement.' His glance skimmed over the neat little lounge before his unfathomable eyes met hers again. She sensed that he had something of importance to say to her, but when he spoke all he asked was, 'You are comfortable here in your quarters?'

'Very comfortable, thank you, *monsieur*,' she replied warily.

'*Bon.*' He glanced down at the book she clutched so tightly to prevent her hands from trembling, and a look of impatience flashed across his lean face. 'I see you have been reading, so I shall not disturb you further. *Bonne nuit.*'

'Goodnight, *monsieur*,' she responded and, when the door closed behind his imposing frame, she lowered herself shakily into the nearest chair.

'I shall not disturb you further,' he had said, but he had, in fact, left her feeling wholly disturbed. She had gained the impression that his visit to her private lounge had not been merely to inform her that she had transgressed from temporary governess to a more permanent position. There had been something else; something which he had considered more important, but he had changed his mind for some reason, and now she was left wondering. She tried to tell herself that she was imagining things, but she had always been able to trust her senses, and the thought persisted that he had intended discussing something rather urgent with her.

Too disturbed now to even think of trying to read, she put down her book and went to bed, but it was a long time before she was relaxed enough to fall asleep.

CHAPTER FOUR

A TOUR of the Royal Botanical Gardens at Pamplemousses was a must, Madame Perreau had told Emma, and on her next free afternoon it was arranged that Li would take Emma there, and that he would call for her again later. The opportunity was one Emma had no intention of missing, and a quiver of excitement rippled through her when she seated herself in the back of Julien Perreau's luxurious car.

The road to Pamplemousses sliced through sugar plantations, and twenty minutes later Li parked the car at the entrance to the botanical gardens where Emma had a perfect view of the gates with the British coat of arms emblazoned on each pillar. Li got out smartly to open the door for her, and Emma stepped eagerly from the air-conditioned interior of the car into the scorching sunshine.

'Thank you, Li,' she smiled, and Li smiled back at her for the first time in all the weeks she had been staying at the villa.

'*Bonjour, mademoiselle.*'

The sound of that suave voice wiped the smile off Li's face, and it made Emma's back stiffen even before she turned to see Louis Villet walking towards them with an almost triumphant look on his handsome face.

'Good afternoon, *monsieur*,' she returned his greeting coldly.

'You are going to visit the gardens?'

'That was the idea,' she replied, tempted now to change her mind.

'Then I shall be your guide,' Louis Villet announced

arrogantly and, before Emma could recover from her astonishment, he turned to Li Ho Kee who stood rigidly beside the open door of the Bentley. 'There is no need to wait, Li. I shall take Mademoiselle Gilbert back to the villa later this afternoon.'

'Very well, *monsieur*,' Li bowed, and moments later he was driving away from the entrance of the gardens.

'You seem to have taken for granted, Monsieur Villet, that I would find pleasure in your company this afternoon,' Emma accused coldly, but his dark eyes continued to smile down into hers.

'I assure you that I am an excellent guide, and please call me Louis.'

'How did you know that I would be coming here this afternoon?' she demanded, ignoring the latter half of his remark.

'I discovered that you have every Wednesday afternoon off, but I arrived at the villa just as you were leaving with Li, so I followed you here in my car.'

'And you naturally assumed that I would fall in with your plans?' she questioned him indignantly.

'You did not object when I dismissed Li,' he pointed out calmly, and Emma could not deny this.

'I was too surprised at your arrogance to do anything,' she explained with some annoyance.

'The English have a saying, Emma, that faint heart never won fair lady,' he mocked her, and everything within her rejected that remark.

'I have no desire to be won, *monsieur*,' she replied bluntly.

'I would not be a man if I did not make the attempt, Emma, and it would please me very much if you would desist from being so unfriendly.' He gestured expressively with his hands as only a Frenchman could do. 'If you continue to call me *monsieur*, then I cannot call you Emma, and Emma is such a nice name.'

His remark awakened her sense of humour, and his face bore such an injured expression that the laughter bubbled up from inside of her to spill from her lips. 'You are impossible.'

'Ah, I have made you laugh, and that is a good sign,' he grinned, and Emma felt herself begin to relax in his company.

'If you're going to be my guide, then I suggest we begin the tour.'

'I am at your service.' He clicked his heels and, taking her hand, he linked her arm with his as they slowly walked up La Bourdonnais avenue: 'The gardens span over sixty acres of ground,' Louis explained. 'Pierre Poivre, a French horticulturist, came out in 1767, and he was the true creator of the gardens. In 1849 a British horticulturist by the name of James Duncan arrived, and he in turn established the collection of palms for which this garden is now famous.'

Emma glanced at him with a suspicion of humour in her eyes. 'You are not by any chance a horticulturist, are you?'

'No, I am in the import and export business,' he enlightened her. 'I am merely interested in the history of this island which is my home.'

They turned off that avenue of palms into another, and paused occasionally for Emma to take photographs.

'There you see the Talipot palms,' Louis pointed, and her glance shifted to the palms with the jagged crisscross effect on their trunks. 'According to legend it flowers only once in a hundred years, but the botanists say it is every sixty years, and it dies once it has flowered.'

'How sad,' she murmured, her glance seeking and finding none of the trees in bloom. 'They are so beautiful.'

'Very beautiful,' Louis agreed, but he was looking at Emma in a manner that suggested a certain intimacy which she chose to ignore as she concentrated on taking photographs.

'Are those nutmeg trees?' she asked excitedly when they had walked a little farther.

'*Oui,*' Louis smiled. 'Pierre Poivre brought nutmeg trees out from the East Indies, and these are examples of the species.' He took her arm and gestured with his free hand. 'If we go this way you can see the lily pond.'

The lily pond lay to the right of an avenue lined with mahogany redwood trees, and her eyes widened at the sight of those giant leaves with their upturned edges. They floated on the water like fluted green flan dishes.

'I have never seen water lilies with such enormous leaves before,' she exclaimed as she stepped up to the edge of the pond.

'It is called the *Victoria amazonica* lily, and it comes from Brazil,' Louis informed her. 'The flowers last only two days. On the first day they are cream-coloured, and on the second day they are pink.'

His tone of voice did not match the excitement she was experiencing, and she glanced up at him guiltily. 'I hope this is not boring you?'

'I am never bored when I am with a beautiful woman.'

His smile was lazy, and his eyes freely roamed her body. She ought to have been annoyed, but instead she was amused by his obvious approach. She had encountered men like him before, and she had no intention of taking him seriously.

'Flattery will get you nowhere, Louis,' she warned.

'The truth is often mistaken for flattery,' he persisted with a careless shrug, and it indicated that his confidence in himself was still in peak form. 'Come, let me show you the Château de Mon Plaisir.'

The trees shaded them from the scorching rays of the sun as they walked up the avenue towards the château, and Louis once again lapsed into an explanation when they paused close to the two-storeyed French colonial house which was now used as offices.

'The original château stood near the main gate, but this building was erected by the British in the 19th century, and it was at one time occupied by that famous British general, Charles Gordon, who was later killed in Khartoum by the Sudanese rebels when they laid siege on the Egyptian capital.'

'Are you sure you're in the import and export business, and that you're not an historian in disguise?' Emma laughed, and he flashed her a brilliant smile which might have disarmed someone who was naïve enough to think he was genuine.

'I am impressing you with my knowledge?'

'Yes, you are,' she admitted wryly, 'and, if I'm not mistaken, that is exactly what you had intended to do.'

'But of course,' he confessed arrogantly, placing his hand lightly on her shoulder and sliding his fingers down the length of her arm to her wrist, but the unwanted familiarity of his caress left her unmoved. 'When a woman is impressed it naturally spices her interest in the one who had impressed her. Not so?'

'Not so,' she contradicted, disengaging her wrist from the clasp of his fingers. 'Some women would find a knowledgeable man like yourself too overwhelming, and it would frighten them away.'

His eyes mocked her. 'You think so?'

'I do.'

'I am not frightening you away, and of that I am sure,' he argued, his glance bold and challenging.

'That is simply because history and botany happen to be my favourite subjects,' she replied with an honesty that made him wince playfully. 'I am also eager to learn, and see as much as I can of your beautiful island.'

'Why do I have the feeling that I am failing in my attempts to establish a closer relationship with you, *chérie*?'

'I'm not interested in the kind of relationship men like yourself usually indulge in.'

He winced again. 'You shatter me, Emma.'

'Why?' she asked, her honesty a weapon against the blatant charm and sensuality which he had hoped would win her over. 'Because I've guessed the truth about you?'

'You intrigue me more and more, Emma,' he told her gravely. 'When I first saw you I realised at once that you are a woman of tender warmth and great passion, it is there in your eyes and in the delightful curve of your mouth, but now I discover that you are also a woman of great intelligence.'

She was not sure whether to take that as a compliment, or to feel embarrassed, but she chose to play safe and ignore it. 'I'm sorry if I have disappointed you.'

'You have not disappointed me, Emma,' Louis smiled, his confidence intact as they approached yet another pond in the gardens. 'You have made me more determined to succeed with you, and I shall find the chase exhilarating.'

'You would be wasting your time,' she warned, tiring of the conversation, and turning from Louis to see a black waterbird fly up into the air from its perch beside the pond. It had a strikingly red beak, and its shrill whinnying call seemed to blend in with the tranquillity of the scene. 'Oh, look!' she cried, pointing.

'That is the Madagascar moorhen,' Louis enlightened her, and they stood there for some time watching the antics of the birds on the pond.

The shadows were lengthening across the rippling water, and Emma glanced at her watch. 'It's getting late, and I must return to the villa.'

Contrary to what she may have imagined, Louis Villet did not argue, and he simply drew her arm through his as he led her from the botanical gardens to where he had parked his BMW.

Emma had been a little nervous about having to drive back to the villa with Louis, but he behaved himself impeccably, and at precisely five minutes to six he parked his car beneath the steps at the entrance to the villa.

'You have found the afternoon pleasant?' he asked, opening the door for her, and she smiled up at him when she stepped out on to the paved driveway.

'Very pleasant,' she admitted. 'Thank you very much, Louis, for being such an informative companion.'

'I will see you again, *chérie*, and soon,' he promised, taking her hand and raising it to his lips. *'Au revoir.'*

Emma stood there until he had driven away, and only then did she walk quickly up the steps, but on the patio she halted abruptly when she came face to face with Julien Perreau where he leaned nonchalantly against the low wall overlooking the garden. She realised at once that the bougainvillaea may have concealed his presence on the patio, but it had also given him a clear view of her arrival at the villa with Louis Villet, and for some inexplicable reason she felt uneasy about it.

'You have spent the afternoon with Louis?' he asked with a casualness that did not evoke suspicion.

'Yes, *monsieur*,' she admitted, her glance taking in the lean, muscled length of him in white linen slacks and blue shirt. No matter what he was wearing, Julien Perreau always succeeded in looking so vitally male that her heart would behave quite irrationally, and this occasion was no exception. 'Monsieur Villet very kindly acted as my guide in the botanical gardens at Pamplemousses.'

Julien Perreau took a packet of his favourite cheroots out of his shirt pocket and, when he lit one, his eyes met hers over the flame of his lighter. 'I hope you know what you are doing, Mademoiselle Emma.'

She was instantly and perhaps unreasonably annoyed. She was not a child, and she did not need Julien Perreau to enlighten her as to the foibles of a man like Louis Villet. She had seen through Louis at their first meeting, but this did not obliterate the fact that she had enjoyed his company that afternoon.

'I know exactly what I am doing,' she said coldly, perhaps a little too coldly, for that lean face became shuttered and granite hard.

'If that is so, then I shall not concern myself with you again,' he announced, turning from her to enter his study, and somehow his remark had had the power to hurt her.

'Monsieur . . .'

'Yes?' he questioned abruptly, pausing to glance at her, but the words seems to dry up in her throat.

What could she say? She had spoken rashly, and by doing so she had rudely dashed away the strange concern he had displayed for her. She felt guilty, and something more which she could not define, but how on earth could she explain this to the harsh-faced, autocratic man who stood waiting with a remarkable show of patience for her to speak.

'It was nothing,' she muttered eventually, an embarrassing warmth flaying her cheeks. 'Excuse me, please.'

She cursed herself all the way up to her suite, but that did not ease the stinging regret that coursed its way through her. The only excuse she could find for her behaviour was that his misplaced concern for her had triggered off the annoyance she had felt for some time because of his total lack of interest in his son, but when she thought about it afterwards she found it a paltry excuse.

Emma did not feel very much like going down to dinner that evening, but to have asked for something to be sent up to her room would only have made matters worse, so she braved the chilly reception she knew she would receive from Julien Perreau, and forced herself to eat a little of the spicy, Oriental meal which had been prepared by the kitchen staff. The silence at the dinner table had never troubled her before, but on this particular evening it made her feel miserable and awkward, and she excused herself as soon as she could to go for a stroll on the beach before going up to bed.

It was a warm night with a near brilliant moon in the sky. It made the sea look as if a million stars had settled on its rippling surface, and the white sand glowed as if it were fluorescent. Emma sighed, it was a perfect night for a stroll on the beach, but she lacked the most important ingredient to make it a perfect night. She needed someone at her side to share in the magical beauty surrounding her, and her mind promptly conjured up a vision of Julien Perreau. She thrust his image from her with an exclamation of annoyance on her lips. It was crazy to think of him at a moment such as this, and she would have to place a much stricter guard on her thoughts in future.

Emma was not sure at what stage during her walk she had become aware of someone lurking in the shadows of the palms along the beach. She had sensed first of all that she was not alone, and later she actually saw a movement in the shadows. Julien Perreau? Ridiculous! He was not the type to lurk in shadows, and neither did he have any reason to do so. Who, then, was following her, and for what reason?

She turned round as casually as possible and walked back the way she had come. Determined not to panic, she forced herself to walk slowly, but knowing that she was being trailed made the fine hair rise in the nape of her neck, and little shivers of fear raced up and down her spine. It was a man, she was certain of that, but he kept his distance, and she hoped that he would continue to do so when she turned towards the path leading up to the villa.

The path was not exceptionally narrow, but it curved up to the villa between an avenue of trees that blanketed out the moonlight. She had never been afraid of walking there before, but on this particular night there was something sinister about the darkness and, knowing that she was being observed, sent an uncommon chill of terror racing through her veins. A twig snapped to the left of her, jarring her nerves, and she automatically quickened her pace, but the next instant a man stepped out into the path directly in front of her. She could not see him clearly in the dappled darkness, for fear was beating against her temples with a force that impaired her vision, but she knew that she would never forget the strong smell of garlic and curry which emanated from him.

Panic took charge of her, activating the muscles in her legs, and she shot past him at a speed which surprised her as much as she imagined it surprised her silent assailant. She heard his heavy footsteps pounding up the path behind her, but she did not slacken her pace even when she heard him drop back.

Barefoot and sandals dangling from her hand, she raced into the villa moments later, and she collided heavily with a solid male body in the hall.

'Mon Dieu!' Julien Perreau exclaimed, his strong arms steadying her and allowing her to lean against him briefly before he held her a little away from him to study her face with a curious expression in his eyes. 'Something has happened to frighten you?'

Heart pounding against her ribs, and her breath rasping in her throat, she stammered, 'Yes—no—I don't know.'

He muttered something unintelligible, and then she was being ushered into his study. 'Sit down,' he ordered.

Aware suddenly that she was shaking all over, she obeyed and, when the padded armchair enfolded her body, she had the ridiculous desire to burst into tears, but she somehow managed to control herself.

'Drink this,' Julien instructed, and when she accepted the glass from him she sniffed at the amber liquid suspiciously.

'What is it?'

A ghost of a smile touched his mouth. 'It is of my best cognac, and it will help to steady your nerves.'

Emma dutifully swallowed down a mouthful, but it almost took her breath away, and there were tears in her eyes when she gasped and raised a hand to her throat. It felt as if she were on fire all the way down into her stomach, but Julien forced her to take another mouthful.

'Enough!' she begged when he would have made her empty the glass. 'This may be your best cognac, but I find it quite revolting.'

'You will feel better in a moment,' was all he said when he took the glass from her, and seconds later the fiery sensation in her stomach began to spread until it steadied the tremors that shook through her.

Realising that she was barefoot, she tried to put on her sandals, but she felt a sharp sting beneath the sole of her right foot which made her draw her breath in sharply between her teeth.

'Let me look at that,' Julien Perreau said and, before

she could protest, he was kneeling on the carpet in front of her, and her foot was being cradled very gently in his well-shaped hands. 'You have a nasty scratch which could turn septic if it is not taken care of at once.'

He lowered her foot carefully to the floor and strode out of his study, but he was back in an instant and kneeling at her feet again. He cleansed the wound and strapped it up securely with elastoplast, and while he did so Emma found herself staring down at his dark head in a dazed fashion. His touch was doing something to her that confused her. Or was it the cognac? She was feeling quite lethargic, and an electrifying, wholly pleasurable sensation was weaving its way through her until she found herself wishing that his careful ministrations would never end.

'Does that feel comfortable?' he asked eventually, snapping shut the metal box he had brought with him, and pushing it aside.

'Very comfortable,' she assured him in a husky voice that sounded quite unlike her own, and he watched her wriggle her toes before he nodded approvingly and rose abruptly to his feet.

'Now, I think, you can tell me what happened out there to frighten you,' he instructed as he placed a cheroot between his lips and cupped his hand around the flame of his lighter.

She felt so safe and secure at that moment that the nasty incident on the beach seemed nothing more than a bad dream, and it was so ridiculous that she wanted to laugh it off, but one look at the stern-faced man observing her through narrowed eyes was enough to make her realise that she owed him an explanation.

'I went for a walk on the beach, which I have done often enough before.'

'That much I have gathered,' he said impatiently

when she paused to recall in her mind every detail of what had occurred.

'Someone followed me,' she blurted out the truth and, when she saw him raise a sceptical eyebrow, she added sharply, 'I'm not lying, and I wasn't imagining it. Someone followed me.'

'You saw this person?'

'Yes ... but unfortunately not very clearly in the darkness.' She bit her lip and shuddered at the memory of what had happened. 'I saw him lurking in the shadow of the trees, and I pretended to be unaware of his presence, but when I came up the path he stepped out in front of me.'

Julien Perreau's jaw hardened. 'He assaulted you?'

'Oh, no!' she shook her head, recalling the smell of garlic and curry which had clung to the man. 'I panicked and ran before he could touch me, or say anything.'

'Was this man perhaps an Indian?'

Emma's head shot up. The question had been asked casually, but she sensed an undercurrent of something which placed her on the alert. 'It's possible that he was an Indian.'

When she thought of the aroma that had emanated from him she decided that is was quite likely that the man had been an Indian, but she was too unsure of herself to make a definite statement to that effect.

'May I suggest that you go to bed and forget all about it,' Julien Perreau interrupted her thoughts, but she did not think that she would ever forget about it entirely.

She got to her feet without bothering to put on her sandals, and they dangled from her fingers when she paused at the door. 'You have been very kind, and I'm grateful. Goodnight, *monsieur*.'

Their eyes met and held for a breathless second, then she turned from him and walked out of his study.

Emma did not sleep very well that night, and she was decidedly jumpy for the next few days until she was able to shift that incident on the beach into the recesses of her mind.

'Look, Emma, look!' Dominic called her excitedly one afternoon when they were in the garden, and she went down on her knees beside him to examine the small reptile sunning itself on the stone-flagged path a little distance from them.

'That's a lizard,' she told him softly.

'*Lézard,*' he laughed delightedly. 'In French it is almost the same . . . *lézard.*'

'*Lézard,*' she repeated, knowing that he was determined she should learn French as he was learning English.

'*Bon, bon!*' he laughed again. 'Now I will say it in English . . . lizard. That is good, yes?'

'That is good,' she agreed, hugging him spontaneously.

They continued their observation of the lizard in silence for a while until the sound of footsteps made them glance up.

'*Papa!* Come and look, *Papa!*' Dominic called his father excitedly, discarding for the first time his reticent manner, but Julien Perreau did not hear him, or perhaps he had not wanted to hear him, for he got into his car and drove away without so much as a glance in their direction. 'He is gone,' Dominic whispered, his expression crestfallen.

'And so is the lizard,' Emma added quietly, her heart aching for the child, but she forced herself to smile brightly, and held out her hand. 'Come, it's time for your bath.'

Dominic accompanied her indoors, but he had closeted himself behind a wall of silence which she could not break through to reach him, and it hurt her to see him like that. He was too young to know the sadness and pain of rejection, and the only way he could cope with it was to shut himself off mentally from everyone around him.

When Emma put Dominic to bed that night he clung to her hand and appeared reluctant to let it go. His tawny eyes looked up into hers, and she sensed a need in him that wrenched at her heart. His lips moved as if he was having difficulty in voicing his thoughts, but he finally spoke in a halting whisper, and she might not have heard the words if she had not been sitting so close to him.

'Je vous aime, Emma. Je vous aime.'

Emma felt an aching lump rise in her throat, but she did not flatter herself that he had truly meant what he had said. This child was absolutely crying out with the need to love and be loved and, since his need was not being fulfilled by those close to him, he was allowing his feelings to spill over on to the most obvious person— herself. Her throat felt tight and her eyes stung, but she knew that she dared not make her observations known to him, for it would seem like yet another rejection.

'I love you too, Dominic,' she whispered, lifting him up and cradling him in her arms with his dark head pressed against her shoulder. 'I love you too.'

She shut her eyes tightly to hold back the tears while she rocked him gently in her arms. She might have said those words initially out of pity and compassion, but, as she held him comfortingly in her arms, she knew that she had spoken from the heart. She had grown more than simply *fond* of Dominic during the past weeks; she had learned to love him, and although it was something she had planned to guard against, she had been incapable of preventing the feelings he had stirred within her.

Emma also felt a fierce anger rising in her. How

could Julien Perreau behave so monstrously towards his own child! How *could* he? When Dominic finally settled down contentedly, Emma resolved that it was time she had a serious discussion with Julien Perreau, and she would do so as soon as the opportunity presented itself.

Julien was not at the dinner table that evening and, when she glanced enquiringly at Madame Perreau, she received the disapproving reply, 'Julien is dining out with Daniella Bertrand this evening, and I was told not to expect him home until late.'

Emma did not comment on this, and Madame Perreau gestured that Nada should serve the first dish. They ate in silence, as if the shadow of Julien's awesome presence lingered in the room even though he was not there, and after dinner Emma followed Celestine's example and retired to her room.

Emma spent an uneasy night contemplating what she had to say to Julien Perreau, and when she awoke the following morning she was more determined than ever to confront him. Dominic's happiness was at stake, and that was of prime importance to her.

They had breakfast out on the terrace as usual and, when Julien finally excused himself to go to his study, Emma knew that this was the opportunity she had been waiting for. She was nervous about it, but there was no sense in delaying it. She excused herself from the table and left Dominic with his grandmother while she followed her employer into the house.

'*Monsieur*, may I have a moment of your time?' she asked a few seconds later when she entered the study without knocking to find Julien Perreau thrusting a wad of important-looking documents into his briefcase, and he looked up, his dark eyes stabbing at her impatiently.

'Is Dominic not behaving himself?'

'Oh, no, *monsieur*, he is absolutely adorable and obedient, but——'

'If he is ill, then he did not appear so at the breakfast table,' Julien interrupted her with undisguised irritation which was beginning to penetrate her calmness and fan the fire of her anger.

'He is in perfect health,' she assured him and, not wanting to waste more of his time than she absolutely had to, she plunged in at the deep end. 'Forgive me, *Monsieur*, but your son needs to know that he still has a father.'

There, she had said it, and now that she had upset the proverbial apple-cart, he could deal with it as he saw fit.

'I know what Dominic needs, *mademoiselle*, and I do not hesitate to give him all that I am capable of giving,' he stated coldly, snapping shut the catches of his briefcase and glancing at his gold wristwatch. 'Now, if you do not mind, I have an appointment at eight-thirty.'

'Dominic doesn't lack the comforts money can buy, but that is not enough,' Emma persisted, determined not to end the matter there when she saw him turn towards the door. 'I have been here more than a month, and not one evening have you taken the trouble to come up to say goodnight to him. That is the least you could do to make him feel loved and wanted.'

'You are there, *mademoiselle*, and I pay you well for your services, do I not?' he asked, his eyes mocking, and his velvety voice icy with sarcasm, then he gestured angrily. 'I cannot stand here discussing this matter when I have a busy schedule ahead of me.'

'Are you too busy to spare a little time occasionally for your own flesh and blood?' she lashed out at him, her eyes flashing with the anger he had aroused. 'Have you no heart, *monsieur*, that you can behave in such an inhuman manner?'

'Inhuman?' he latched on to the word, his dark eyes

narrowed slits of fury as they raked her derisively from head to foot. 'You say I am inhuman?'

Emma trembled inwardly. She had gone too far, perhaps, but now there was no going back, and she raised her chin with a gesture of defiance. 'How else am I to interpret the callous way you treat Dominic. You ignore his existence except when it pleases you, and on occasions such as that you treat him like a casual acquaintance instead of your own son. A child needs much more than that, *monsieur*, and if I can't make you understand that, then you *are* inhuman.'

'*Inhuman! Mon Dieu!*' His features, dark and dangerous, instilled a fear that chilled her almost to the marrow as he flung his briefcase on to a chair. He lessened the distance between them with a few lithe strides until he stood towering over her, and he looked for all the world like a volcano about to erupt. 'I will show you what is inhuman, *mademoiselle*!'

She had expected a verbal lashing from this autocratic, often emotionless man, but she was totally unprepared for the agonising grip of his hands on her shoulders as he jerked her up against the rock-hard length of his body. The shock of it robbed her of the breath to cry out in protest, and she caught a panic-stricken glimpse of his cruelly twisted lips before his mouth descended on hers with a savagery that crushed her lips against her teeth.

Emma felt the sting of tears behind her closed eyelids. She tried to push him away with her hands against his chest, but he was immovable, and he did not release her until the fiery anger of his kiss had ignited an answering fire in her that made her go limp against him.

'*Mon Dieu!*' he muttered, pushing her away from him, and Emma despised herself as she clutched blindly at the chair close to her to steady her swaying, trembling body, but one look at the grim set of his jaw told her that he despised himself even more.

'*Mon Dieu!*' Julien exploded once again, and moments later she was alone in his study with a head that was spinning, and lips that felt as if the imprint of his hard mouth would remain there for the rest of her life.

CHAPTER FIVE

IF Emma could have kept her anger alive, then it might have sustained her throughout the day, but instead her encounter with Julien Perreau that morning had left her feeling confused and somewhat guilty. She had been led by her determination to help Dominic, but in the process she had made matters worse. Instead of approaching the situation tactfully, she had blundered in, and her confrontation with her employer had ended in disaster. She ought to have been sacked on the spot, but instead Julien Perreau had reacted in a most unexpected way. When she fingered her lips they still felt tender, and his strong hands had left bruises on her shoulders which she kept hidden beneath the short sleeves of her blouse. She shuddered at the memory of his anger, and she could not forget the fire he had ignited within her which had left her trembling and emotionally disturbed. She had been kissed before and left unmoved, but she would never have believed that a man's angry kisses could leave her shaken to the very core of her being.

Emma dreaded having to face him again, but living under the same roof made avoiding him quite impossible. He had had every right to be angry with her and, when they met at the dinner table that evening, her heart thudded at the realisation of what she had to do. He acknowledged her presence with a curt nod, then he ignored her, but Emma's awareness of him had her nerve ends quivering in a way which robbed her almost totally of her appetite. Her hands trembled, and remorse sat like a lump in her throat which forced her to excuse herself from the table before the dessert was served.

Later, when she stood at her bedroom window, she saw the light go on in his study and spread its glow across the otherwise darkened patio. Now! She had to go to him *now*. She had known all day that this moment would come, and she could not shy away from it like a coward.

Emma left her room and went downstairs before she could change her mind, but her courage almost failed her when she stood facing the door to his study. The rapid, nervous beat of her heart almost choked her, and her hand was shaking visibly when she tapped lightly on the panelled door.

'*Entrez,*' he instructed abruptly, and the metal handle felt cold against her hot, damp palm when she turned it and opened the door to take a hesitant step into the study.

Julien Perreau was seated behind his desk with his white shirt unbuttoned almost to his waist, and his cold, unwelcome eyes sent her nervous glance skidding downwards to where a crucifix on a silver chain nestled among the short dark hair on his tanned chest. There was not an ounce of superfluous flesh on his lean, muscular body, and she felt her insides tremble at the memory of its hardness against her own.

'May I have a word with you, please, *monsieur*?' she asked, and she was surprised at how calm and confident her voice sounded.

'Come in and close the door,' he commanded, and she obeyed him at once, but the words seemed to wither in her throat when she stood facing him across the cluttered expanse of his desk. Awkward seconds elapsed in silence, then he raised a quizzical eyebrow. 'You have something you wish to say?'

'I—I had no right to—to criticise you this morning,

monsieur,' she stumbled into stammering speech, then she pulled herself together sharply. 'I owe you an apology.'

'You accused me of being inhuman, *mademoiselle*, but I think it is the discovery that I am human after all which has brought you here to me.' Emma made no attempt to hide her confusion when he got up behind his desk and walked round it to stand towering over her. 'Perhaps you wish for more of this?'

Emma had sensed the danger, but the knowledge that her innocent and honest apology could be twisted out of context had rendered her immobile in disbelief, and she was too numb with disappointment to resist when his arms locked about her. His hard mouth settled on hers, not brutally this time, but with a sensual force that drove her lips apart. She held herself rigid and impassive in the circle of his hard arms, but the feel of his lean, male body against her own was doing things to her she had never dreamed of before, and a natural response rose within her which she was still coherent enough to know had to be suppressed. Anger came to her rescue, and she raised her hands, encountering warm, hair-roughened flesh as she pushed him away from her, and he let her go.

Her heart was pounding, and her insides were shaking with a multitude of emotions she could not even begin to analyse. If any other man had insulted her in this way she might have resorted to slapping his face, but Julien Perreau was her employer, and she very much wanted to maintain her position as governess to his small son.

'I can understand and forgive you for doing that this morning, *monsieur*,' she said coldly, and with admirable calmness, 'but this time you have not only made a mockery of my apology, you have sought to humiliate me, and that I cannot forgive.'

She glimpsed the tightening of his mouth when she brushed past him and marched towards the door, but he was there before her, his shoulder against the door to prevent her from opening it, and his hand gripping her arm to detain her. Angry words hovered on her lips, but, when she looked up into his dark, smouldering eyes, she felt her anger drain away from her to leave her empty and peculiarly vulnerable.

'Emma . . .' The deep, dusky velvet of his voice when he spoke her name sent a shiver of something close to pleasure through her, but before he could say more the telephone on his desk started ringing shrilly, and the sound seemed to jar him as much as it did her.

'You had better answer it, *monsieur*,' she said quietly, and only then did he release her arm and move away from her.

'*Mon Dieu!*' he muttered almost savagely. 'We will continue this discussion later.'

Not if I can help it, she thought frantically as she fled from his study, and in the process she almost collided with Madame Perreau on the stairs.

'Emma?' Her shrewd glance did not miss the unnatural fire in Emma's blue eyes. 'My son has angered you?'

'No, *madame*, it is my own stupidity which angers me,' Emma retorted, realising that she had achieved none of what she had set out to do. 'Goodnight, *madame*.'

She was aware of the older woman's quizzical glance following her up the stairs, but she was too emotionally disturbed at that moment to stop and explain.

Alone in her room, when she was considerably calmer, she realised that her attempt to make her employer aware of his son's needs had had about as much effect as an enraged ram battering a concrete wall. He could not, or *would* not understand, and her ill-chosen words in a moment of anger had aroused an unexpected savagery in him that morning, but this evening's confrontation had ended in a fiasco of a different nature. Oh, *why* could she not have left well alone? she asked herself, but when she thought of Dominic she knew that she *could* not leave the matter there. Dominic needed his father, and the love and understanding only a father could give, and she would do something about it even if it killed her.

It was not Dominic who dominated her thoughts when she lay in bed that night, but Julien Perreau. He had deliberately twisted her apology into something with which he could humiliate her, but she realised now that it was not humiliation she had felt when he had held her in his arms. She had known a vague longing to remain close to him, and to surrender herself to the feelings which had begun to stir within her. Shocked at herself, she turned over on to her stomach and buried her hot face in the pillow.

'This is crazy,' she muttered to herself in the darkness. 'I'm being affected by the heat here in the tropics, or otherwise I need to have my head read.'

Emma awoke the following morning with the sensation that she had been closeted in a soundproof room. It was only when she was fully awake that she realised the birds were not warbling in the trees outside her window, and their absence filled her with a strange uneasiness which increased when she took Dominic down to breakfast. Both Julien and his mother had an edgy look about them which she found difficult to fathom, and twice she caught Julien glancing up at the clear blue sky as if he saw something there that remained invisible to her.

'Why is everything so quiet this morning, as if the whole world is holding its breath prior to an explosion?' the query finally spilled from Emma's lips before she could prevent it and, surprisingly, it was Julien who answered her.

'You are quite right,' he said. 'This is what is called the calm before the storm, and I mean that literally.'

'But there's not a cloud in sight,' she protested, lowering her knife and fork to gaze up at the sky with her eyes narrowed against the sun. 'There can't possibly be a storm brewing.'

'I would like to believe that myself, *mademoiselle*,' he smiled faintly, 'but the absence of the birds this morning is a sign I cannot ignore.'

Cyclone! The word leapt unbidden into Emma's mind, but she thrust it from her instantly, and rebuked herself silently for anticipating the worst. It was a known fact that Mauritius was prone to cyclones during the summer months from December to February, but Emma could not believe that this unnatural calmness was the forerunner of something so violent and destructive.

It was during Dominic's English lesson that Emma noticed the ominous clouds building up, and the wind had risen to chase them more swiftly across the sky until the sun was blotted out. Dominic glanced up at Emma, and she imagined that he was thinking similar thoughts of impending disaster, but she maintained a calm expression and continued with the lesson.

The weather became steadily worse as the day progressed, but there was still no sign of anything more than a normal thunderstorm. At the dinner table that evening Julien suggested that the louvers outside the windows be fastened securely, and when Emma went to bed that night she made sure that Dominic's windows, as well as her own, were securely shuttered.

The storm erupted shortly after ten that night. Gale force winds tore across the island, and rain battered ferociously against the shuttered windows. The lights went out as if someone had flicked the switches, and somewhere close to her suite a louver was banging loudly. Emma slipped out of bed, and fumbled in the darkness for her silk robe, then she followed the sound into Dominic's room.

'Emma!' he cried panic-stricken when he saw her enter his darkened room, but she had to see to the louver before she could pause to comfort him.

The catch had worked its way loose in the wind which tugged savagely at the wooden louver like a giant hand intent upon tearing it from its hinges.

'It's all right, Dominic,' she tried to pacify the child while she battled against the wind and the rain which was coming in through the open window to beat against her face. When the wind released its hold on the louver for one fraction of a second, Emma slipped the catch into position, and she almost cried with relief when she pulled down the window to shut out the elements of nature.

'Emma, I am frightened,' Dominic whimpered when she felt her way towards him and, disregarding the dampness of her face and her robe, she scooped him up into her arms when she sat down on his bed.

'Don't be frightened, darling,' she said quietly, pressing his head into her shoulder in an attempt to shield him from the sound of the howling wind and the rain. 'I'll stay here with you until the storm is over.'

Dominic's hands clutched at her as if she were a safe port in a hurricane, and she was sitting with her head bowed over him when the bedroom door opened abruptly behind her.

'Papa!' Dominic cried when he looked up to see Julien entering the room carrying an oil lamp, but he did not release his hold on Emma who was having difficulty controlling her wayward heart at the sight of the man approaching the bed.

'Do not be afraid, Dominic,' he spoke, comfortingly, his hand briefly touching the child's head, then he placed the lamp on the bedside cupboard and directed his dark gaze at Emma. 'It is a cyclone, but fortunately it is not passing directly over the island.'

Cyclone. The word should have struck terror into her heart, but instead she felt quite safe with Julien Perreau there in the room with her.

'Do you think it will be over soon?' she asked, taking in his lean length which was still fully clothed in the grey slacks and blue shirt he had worn at dinner.

'It is moving quite fast.'

'Will you stay with us, *Papa*?' Dominic asked in a wavering voice, his tawny gaze raised pleadingly to his father's.

'I will stay, *mon enfant*,' Julien smiled with a show of affection Emma had not witnessed in the weeks she had been taking care of Dominic, and an undeniable warmth stole into her heart as she watched Julien pull up a chair and seat himself close to the bed.

Dominic leaned contentedly against Emma while the cyclone continued to rage outside, and she had no concept of time as they sat there in silence. The violence of the cyclone had slowly abated, and it was Julien who eventually made her aware of what a weight Dominic had become in her arms.

'He is asleep,' Julien said softly, and Emma looked down into the child's sleeping face with some surprise.

'Yes, so he is,' she whispered, lowering him on to the bed, and her arms felt a little stiff when she covered him gently with the sheet while Julien doused the light.

Dominic stirred briefly in his sleep, then he was still, and a strong hand at Emma's elbow propelled her quietly out of the room.

In the lamp-lit passage, before they reached the door to her suite, the tightening of Julien's hand on her elbow made her turn to glance up at him, and his eyes burned down into hers with a strange fire that had the oddest effect on her pulse rate.

'You are trembling,' he observed, taking her by the shoulders, and she could actually feel herself shaking beneath his hands.

'I guess I found the cyclone more frightening than I imagined, *monsieur*,' she confessed unsteadily, and this was not altogether a lie, but she was beginning to think that she was frightened more by the strange vibrations emanating from Julien Perreau.

He was exuding a strong and irresistible magnetism which held her spellbound, and oddly breathless, and there was not one iota of resistance in her trembling body when his hands slid across her shoulder blades to draw her up against him. Her head seemed to tilt forward of its own volition to rest on his broad chest, and he held her with a strange gentleness that made the blood skip faster through her veins. The clean male smell of him overwhelmed her senses as nothing had ever done before, and a weakness surged into her limbs that made her thankful for the steely strength of his body to lean against.

'There is no longer any need to be afraid, *ma chérie*,' the velvety smoothness of his voice soothed her and, driven by a force too strong to resist, her arms circled his lean waist, and she raised her face to his with an undeniable, yet unconscious invitation of her parted, quivering lips.

Emma heard him draw a quick breath, then he set his mouth on hers in a light, almost exploratory caress which lasted less than a second, but it was sufficient to awaken a need within her which was echoed in the hardening of his body against hers. His mouth captured hers again, and this time he kissed her with a sensual expertise that sent a piercingly sweet stab of emotion through her. Her lips responded to the intimacy of his kiss with a knowledge she had not known she possessed, and the muscles in his back were quiveringly taut beneath her palms when she slid her hands up to his broad shoulders to cling to him weakly.

His fingers bit into her waist, then his hands slid upwards until they cupped the swell of her breasts through the silk of her robe, and for the first time in her life she did not shy away from this intimate caress, but actually revelled in it. She would never have believed that any man could succeed in making her feel so ecstatically alive that every nerve in her body would quiver in response to his touch and his kisses, but Julien Perreau was doing just that, and her eyes were stormy with the emotions he had aroused when he released her abruptly.

'*Mon Dieu!*' he muttered thickly, and his face was pale when his hands went out once again to steady her as she swayed weakly towards him. '*Pardon, mademoiselle*, I had no right to do that.'

Emma could not believe that she was hearing correctly. It was like a douche of iced water in the face, and she came to her senses with a painful jar to see him striding away from her. Humiliation stung her cheeks, and she entered her suite blindly, bumping into the lounge furniture in the darkness until she reached her bedroom.

'Dear heaven, what have I done?' she breathed shakily, and her legs gave way beneath her so that she sat down rather heavily on the bed. She could still feel the sensual warmth of his mouth against hers, and the gentle caress of his hands against her breasts, but a wave of shame washed over her to make a mockery of that brief, magical moment. What had she done? The answer was only too glaringly obvious. In a moment of something close to insanity she had invited his kisses, and he had reacted like any other man confronted with such a temptation. Emma cringed inwardly, but there was yet another glaring truth staring her in the face, and she could not ignore it no matter how much she tried. She had unintentionally poached on Daniella Bertrand's territorial grounds, and Daniella would consider that quite unforgivable. Is that what Julien had meant when he had said that he had no right to kiss her? And would he confide his lapse in Daniella? Emma felt herself shrinking at the thought, and she groaned as she fell across her bed to bury her hot face in her pillow. Would she ever live this down? And how was she going to face him again in the cold light of day after the way she had behaved?

Her mind cruelly gave her no peace. In the grey light of dawn she was still awake, and dreading the day ahead of her.

The cyclone may not have passed directly over the island, but it had left a considerable amount of damage in its wake. The Mauritians were, however, accustomed to dealing with such emergencies. The power was swiftly restored, and so also the telephone communications. Celestine Perreau's face wore a resigned expression at the breakfast table, but it nearly broke Emma's heart to witness the havoc which the cyclone had created in the villa's beautiful garden. Leaves and flower petals lay scattered all over the place, branches of trees had snapped, and some of Li's prize roses had been twisted and ripped completely out of the soil.

'Li will soon have it in perfect order again,' Celestine assured Emma, and Emma found herself wondering how Li would cope with such an enormous task, but later that morning a half dozen men arrived from the Perreau sugar plantation, and between them they swiftly cleared away the debris.

Julien had left for Tamarin early that morning to

assess the damage at the hotel, and Emma was relieved to know that she would not have to face him until that evening, but she need not have been concerned. Julien was once again the aloof, autocratic employer, and he made it easy for her to believe that she had simply lived through a bad dream.

Nada interrupted Dominic's English lesson one morning a few days later to summon Emma to the telephone, and Emma's heart shot into her mouth. She had given the villa's telephone number to Lucy in case of an emergency, and her immediate thought was that something unpleasant had happened.

She made sure that Dominic had something to keep himself occupied with, then she raced downstairs into the hall, and snatched up the receiver.

'Emma Gilbert speaking,' she said a little breathlessly into the mouthpiece.

'Ah, Emma, *chérie*, it is so good to hear your voice again.'

Emma sighed inwardly with relief and a great deal of annoyance. 'Good-morning, Louis.'

'How cold you sound, Emma,' he accused mockingly. 'Are you not pleased to hear from me?'

'I am a little surprised,' she confessed as she leaned against the wall and felt her frightened heartbeats subside.

'You thought I had forgotten you?'

'I never gave you a thought at all,' she answered bluntly and truthfully, and Louis groaned at the other end as if she had struck him physically.

'How brutally unkind you are, *chérie*, when I have done nothing but think of you day and night since our last meeting.'

'Am I supposed to be impressed?'

'But of course!' he brightened. 'It is not often that I spend so many hours thinking of one woman only.'

Emma almost laughed out loud, but she stifled the sound before it reached her lips. Louis was smooth, very smooth, and she might have believed him if she had not seen through him at their first meeting. 'What can I do for you, Louis?'

'Have dinner with me this evening?'

The invitation was unexpected, and a blunt refusal sprang to her lips, but she realised in time that perhaps the occasion called for a little diplomacy. 'I'm afraid that is out of the question.'

'Why?' he shot the question at her, obviously not satisfied unless he received a reasonable explanation for her refusal.

'I'm not free in the evenings,' she lied.

'But surely, *chérie*, you do not have to sit and hold Dominic's hand all night?' Louis protested strongly.

'I must be here if he should need me,' she explained, wishing he would not be so persistent.

'Make this evening an exception?' Louis pleaded, and Emma found that her defences were wearing thin.

'I shall have to ask Monsieur Perreau's permission, and I doubt if I shall see him before this evening,' she tried to put him off, but she was fast becoming acquainted with Louis' determination.

'Do not let that concern you. I will arrange it for you with Julien,' he announced, taking it for granted that she would agree. 'Be ready at seven, *chérie. Au revoir.*'

'But Louis . . .' The line went dead with a decisive 'click', and Emma was left holding a lifeless receiver.

A wave of exasperation and annoyance swept through her, and she slammed down the receiver with an unnecessary force before she went upstairs to resume Dominic's lesson.

Emma hoped fervently that Julien would not give her the evening free to dine with Louis, but when he arrived at the villa late that afternoon he came directly up to her suite to confront her.

'I believe Louis has invited you out to dinner this evening,' he said abruptly, declining her invitation to enter her lounge, and making her feel as if she was about to commit a crime.

'Yes, *monsieur*, but I——'

'I did say you could have an evening free when you wished, but I hope you are not going to make a habit of it?' he interrupted her explanation contemptuously, and her chin rose in defiance and anger.

'I have no intention of shirking my responsibilities where Dominic is concerned, *monsieur*.'

'I am happy to hear that,' he announced, his dark eyes raking her coldly from head to foot before he turned on his heel and strode away.

Emma stood there for a moment with a mixture of feelings racing through her. Could this really be the man who had held her so comfortingly in his arms that night after the cyclone had passed, or had she truly imagined the tender passion of his kisses?

She pulled herself together with an effort and closed the door. For her own peace of mind she knew that it would be safer not to dwell on what had happened that night. It stirred up feelings best forgotten, and incidents which still had the power to fill her with shame.

Her black evening dress was perhaps a bit severe, she decided some time later when she studied herself in the mirror, but she was in a rather severe mood, and not looking forward at all to her dinner engagement with Louis. What she did not notice was that the simplicity in the style of her dress accentuated the creamy smoothness of her tanned shoulders, and the slender, enchanting curve of breasts and hips. The light above the dressing table highlighted the golden sheen of her brown hair, and it cast a provocative shadow between her breasts. The saleslady had assured her that it was quite decent, but Emma had always found the cut of the bodice too low for comfort. The dress had looked good in the boutique's dressing-room, but somehow she had never had the nerve to wear it to any function to which she had been invited. This evening, however, she was not in the mood for gay colours, and the black dress would have to suffice, daring neck-line and all.

'Chérie, you look *superbe!*' Louis boosted her morale when he collected her precisely at seven that evening.

'Thank you,' she murmured, not quite sure whether she ought to feel flattered when she saw his eyes linger a moment on her breasts. Moments later she was comfortably seated in his BMW and they were driving away from the villa when Emma glanced at Louis enquiringly. 'Where are we going?'

The dashboard light illuminated the smile on his handsome face. 'Have you been yet to Belle Mare?'

'No, I haven't.'

'That is where we are going,' he announced, 'and I can give you my word that the food is of the best.'

'I'm sure it is,' Emma replied without much enthusiasm.

'Do you like dancing?' Louis questioned her when the silence threatened to lengthen between them.

'I can't really say.' An unwilling smile plucked at her mouth when she thought of her past attempts at those often intricate steps on the dance floor. 'I'm not very good at it.'

'I will teach you,' he announced with amusing confidence.

'It seems to me that besides being a historian and a botanist you are also a ballroom dancing instructor.'

'Ah, you mock me, *chérie*, and that is not very nice,' he smiled ruefully as he glanced at her briefly.

'I refuse to take you seriously, Louis.'

'But with you I am very serious,' he insisted, triggering off her sense of humour.

'That's what you say to every woman you meet,' she accused laughingly.

'You are being unkind again.'

Emma stared at the twin beams of light slicing through the darkness, and for some inexplicable reason she felt a wave of sadness surging through her. 'The truth is sometimes unkind.'

'I have never met a woman before who has presented me with such a challenge, and I am finding it very stimulating.' A silence settled between them which lasted several seconds, then he enquired humorously, 'You have nothing to say to that?'

'You will turn whatever I say to your advantage,' she informed him, but the smile in her voice lightened the accusation, and he threw back his sleek head and laughed an attractive, deep-throated laugh.

If only Julien would laugh sometimes. The thought leapt unbidden into her mind, but she thrust it out just as swiftly. She did not want to think about Julien Perreau. Not tonight! Her determination had always come to her assistance in the past, but on this occasion she could not shut out the image of his lean, striking features. His eyes, mocking and contemptuous at times, taunted her mercilessly, and she was forced to remember how she had invited his kisses that night in the lamp-lit passage during the aftermath of the cyclone. Oh, God, would she never live down her shame? She had never invited a man's kisses before, and she could only think that she had been overcome by some sort of madness, for madness it had most certainly been.

'There is the hotel,' Louis interrupted her disturbing thoughts, and she made an effort to show an interest.

The hotel, well-lit at night, seemed to cover several

acres of ground along the coast. It was, she discovered, a holiday resort which catered for almost every whim a visitor could have from sport to an all-night casino, and added to that there was an attractive stretch of beach where one could sunbathe, swim, surf, or ski.

The pillared arches and tiled floor reminded her of ancient Arabic architecture, and she secretly wished she could linger in the foyer to admire it more closely. Sun-bronzed visitors lounged in comfortable chairs, or tried their luck at the gambling tables in the casino, but Emma had only a brief glimpse of the latter as Louis led her towards the restaurant where a band was lustily providing music for the guests who wished to dance.

The chief steward seemed to know Louis. He smiled and bowed politely as he murmured, 'This way, please, Monsieur Villet.'

'I did not book a table for four,' Louis protested when they stood beside a table in a secluded alcove.

'I took the liberty of making a slight adjustment to your table booking, *mon ami*,' a familiar voice spoke directly behind Emma, and both she and Louis swung round to find themselves confronted by Julien Perreau with a ravishing Daniella Bertrand clinging to his arm. 'I was certain you would not object if Daniella and I joined you this evening,' Julien explained smoothly.

His mocking glance shifted from Louis to Emma, and his dark eyes burned their way down the length of her and up again to her flushed face. She had so desperately wanted to avoid thinking about Julien that his unexpected appearance in the restaurant was almost tragic, and she was caught somewhere between the desire to laugh and cry.

'You are quite right, Julien,' Louis announced without so much as batting an eyelid. 'I do not mind at all.'

They sat down, and Julien ordered wine as if the

evening ahead had been arranged solely by him. Emma smothered her suspicions and glanced at the woman seated opposite her. Red was a colour which had never suited Emma, but on Daniella Bertrand it was a perfect foil for her dark, latin looks, and Emma suspected that she was perfectly aware of this. They smiled at each other politely, but without warmth, and Emma got the feeling that Daniella considered it beneath her dignity to have to dine with one of Julien's employees.

The conversation did not get down to a scintillating start, but then Emma could not recall Julien ever being talkative at the dinner table. Or was it only at the villa that he had no desire to communicate during the evening meal?

The music was loud, too loud at times, and Emma found herself viewing her first evening out with a wariness that made her feel rigid and uncomfortable.

CHAPTER SIX

THE hotel restaurant's speciality that evening was seafood, superbly prepared and served, but Emma could not do justice to the prawns she had ordered. She was too aware of Julien Perreau's lean, muscular presence so close to her, and every time their eyes happened to meet she was conscious of little shock waves coursing through her. She was aware also of Daniella Bertrand's slender hand resting on his arm from time to time, and the easy familiarity with which she did so was stabbing at Emma in a way she dared not stop to analyse.

The atmosphere around the table might have been awkward and tense if it had not been for Louis' charming and bracing personality. Emma had expected him to sulk because his plans had gone awry, but he did nothing of the sort, and neither did he mention it on the few occasions he had asked Emma to dance. His style of dancing was polished and smooth, but his steps were easy to follow, and Emma actually enjoyed herself when she did not glance at Julien and Daniella gliding slowly across the floor in time to the music.

'Do you think we could sit this one out?' Emma asked Louis when the waltz ended and was followed at once by a tango.

'*Bien sûr.*' They returned to their table with his arm draped lightly about her waist, and they sat there in companionable silence sipping their wine until Julien and Daniella danced past them. It was then, for the first time that evening, that Emma saw Louis scowl. 'There would be little I would not give to know how Julien found out I would be bringing you here this evening,' he muttered.

'I thought you said that you didn't mind,' she teased lightly, and he gestured expressively with his hands.

'There are times when one must admit defeat.'

'And tonight is one of those times?'

'*Précisément!*' he nodded, lighting a cigarette with obvious agitation, and she could not help feeling vaguely amused.

'I must admit, Louis, you accepted your defeat very gallantly.'

'You were impressed?' he shot the question at her eagerly while he observed her through a haze of smoke, and Emma had difficulty in keeping a straight face.

'I was very impressed.'

Louis leaned forward to study her more closely. 'You are laughing at me, I can see it in your eyes.'

'I'm not laughing at you,' she assured him hastily, 'but I couldn't resist teasing you a little.'

'*Mon Dieu!* ... I shall not forgive Julien very easily for tonight,' he scowled, his dark eyes scanning the dance floor, then he changed the subject abruptly. 'They look good together, do they not?'

'Yes,' she agreed with an odd tightness in her throat when her gaze followed his to where Julien and Daniella were dancing close together.

Daniella threw her head back at that moment to smile up at Julien with a provocativeness which was quite suited to the latin dance, and Emma felt a stab of something close to jealousy when Julien smiled back at Daniella.

'Good heavens, what's the matter with me?' she asked herself angrily, but the answer skilfully eluded her, and the next moment Louis was saying something which swiftly altered the train of her thoughts.

'They have been very close these past two years, and

Daniella Bertrand is a very attractive woman, but she is not—how do you say—my cup of tea.'

Daniella Bertrand was an extremely attractive woman, Emma could not deny that, but it was what Louis had said initially which stirred her curiosity to the point where she could no longer keep silent.

'Louis . . .' she began hesitantly, and when she gained his attention she asked the question which had been troubling her almost from the moment she had arrived in Mauritius. 'Why is it that there are no photographs at the villa of Monsieur Perreau's late wife, and why is her name never mentioned?'

Louis drew hard on his cigarette and crushed the remainder into the ashtray as if he were crushing the memory of something unpleasant. 'After Marguerite's death Julien destroyed all her photographs, and her name is not mentioned because Julien has forbidden it.'

Emma drew a shocked breath. 'But why?'

'I cannot tell you, *chérie*,' Louis said, and his glance darted almost guiltily in Julien's direction.

Emma felt the stirring of a pain deep down inside of her. 'Did he love her so very much that he can't bear even to have her name mentioned?'

'Love her?' Louis looked startled, almost amused, then he laughed harshly. 'Julien did not love his wife . . . he despised her.'

Emma felt the shock of that statement like a physical blow to the central part of her nervous system, and it left her numb and speechless. It could not be true, could it? She stared at Louis, but his face had become strangely shuttered, and she was forced to leave the matter there when she glimpsed Julien and Daniella returning to the table.

She could not look at Julien, and she jumped at the chance to get away for a moment to sort herself out when Daniella suggested going to the cloakroom. Julien had despised his wife! *Impossible!* Louis was prone to exaggeration, and it would be quite in character for him to exaggerate in this instance. But *why*?

'Louis was not very pleased at the thought that Julien and I would be dining with you this evening,' Daniella cut into Emma's turbulent thoughts.

'I realise that,' Emma smiled stiffly while she touched up her lipstick, and she wondered if anyone had noticed the suggestion of paleness in her cheeks.

'I thought it was quite ridiculous of Julien to want to come here this evening to act as chaperon,' Daniella continued, her heavily lashed eyes meeting Emma's speculatively in the mirror. 'You are not a child, and I am of the opinion that you know exactly what you are doing.'

Her tone of voice suggested something which Emma was finding distasteful, and an icy anger surged through ehr that awakened the devil inside her.

'Where men like Louis are concerned, I always know what I'm doing,' Emma agreed, deciding that Daniella could make of that what she wished, and the triumphant smile curving those crimson lips told Emma that Daniella was doing exactly that.

'Then I shall tell Julien so,' she announced, sounding like a child threatening to tell her mother of someone else's misdemeanour.

'Please do,' Emma snapped, putting away her lipstick and walking out of the cloakroom ahead of Daniella Bertrand.

The restaurant was beginning to feel airless, and Emma was more than ready to leave, but when they reached their table Julien rose and placed his hand on Emma's arm to prevent her from sitting down.

'I am sure, Louis, you will not object if I have this dance with Mademoiselle Emma?' he queried, taking Emma's purse from her trembling fingers and placing it on the table.

'I do not mind at all, *mon ami*,' Louis announced, rising to his feet and extending his hand gallantly towards Daniella. 'Perhaps, Daniella, you will do me the honour this once of dancing with me?'

Daniella did not refuse, and Emma was left with no choice but to allow Julien to lead her on to the floor. She did not feel like dancing with him, the mere thought of it set her nerves jangling, and her body felt as rigid as the carved pillars at the entrance to the hotel.

Julien's hand was resting in the hollow of her back, his light touch stirring up vibrations she could not ignore, and somehow she found herself matching her steps to his as he guided her across the crowded floor. He held her a comfortable distance away from him, but it still allowed him to guide her expertly into the variations of the dance and, incredibly, she began to relax and enjoy herself.

'You have enjoyed the evening, *mademoiselle*?' he spoiled her enjoyment with that hateful mockery in his voice, and her body stiffened automatically.

'Very much, *monsieur*,' she lied.

'Perhaps I should give you more freedom in the evenings if you are finding life here on the island a little dull for your taste,' he suggested cynically, and her anger rose sharply.

'Life on Maritius has not been dull at all and, if I had wanted more freedom in the evenings, I would have asked for it,' she announced coldly.

'You are annoyed at my concern, but I assure you it was never my intention to chain you to my son's side.'

'I never imagined that you——'

She halted abruptly, catching her breath when Julien pulled her up against his hard body to avoid bumping into someone else, and the unexpected contact with his lean, muscled frame sent a charge of electrified emotions darting through her that left her considerably shaken.

'*Pardon*, you were saying?' he reminded her when he held her away from him again, but her thoughts were scattered like the debris after the recent cyclone, and her heart was beating so hard and fast that she could scarcely breathe.

'I—I was——' Her hand tightened involuntarily on his shoulder when her steps faltered, and she knew with sudden clarity that it would be fatal to continue this dance with him. 'Please, *monsieur*, would you mind very much if we returned to our table?'

'You are very pale,' he observed, his dark eyes studying her intently and, when she did not comment, he placed his arm more firmly about her waist. 'It is stifling in here, and I think what we both need is a little fresh air.'

Emma felt too curiously weak to protest as he guided her towards the exit, but she welcomed the warm, fresh night air when they stepped out on to the terrace. The breeze brushed against her cold cheeks and playfully lifted the hair against her temples as Julien took her down the steps on to the deserted beach where the palms were casting deep shadows in the moonlight.

'This is very much better, is it not?' he asked, his hand firm and warm beneath her elbow.

'Yes ... thank you,' she gulped nervously.

If only her heart would stop racing like a mad thing, and if only he would not walk so close to her. The sand was getting into her silver sandals, and she grimaced at the discomfort. Sandals were not exactly the ideal shoes to wear for a late night stroll on the beach, but then she had not envisaged anything like this, and neither had she imagined that it would be with Julien Perreau.

They paused close to the water's edge, and only then did he release her arm to light one of his favourite, aromatic cheroots. 'I have given some thought to your accusations that I do not spend time with Dominic, and——'

'Oh, please, *monsieur*, can't we simply forget——'

'*Non!*' He raised an imperious hand to silence her, and in the moonlit darkness he looked sterner and more autocratic than ever before. 'It was wrong of you to criticise me without understanding the circumstances, but there was some truth in what you said. I have not been making time for my son these past two years and, although you may not think so, it is something which grieves me.'

There it was again! *These past two years.* Why couldn't he simply say: *Since my wife's death!* Was that so difficult?

Steering her thoughts back to what he had said, she asked: 'Why haven't you done something about it, then?'

The tip of his cheroot glowed red in the darkness when he drew on it. 'If I told you that my actions have been motivated by the desire to save Dominic further pain, would that suffice?'

Emma shook her head. 'No, *monsieur*, it would not. Your uncaring behaviour towards him is causing him a great deal more pain than you will ever realise. He desperately needs to know that you care; he *craves* it, and if you really have any feeling for him, then I suggest you make an attempt to show it.'

'And what if he is hurt again?'

Emma hesitated, she was treading on unfamiliar ground and, for Dominic's sake, she dared not risk making a false move. 'I can't pretend to understand what you are referring to, *monsieur*,' she said at length, 'but I do know that children can overcome almost anything if they know that they are loved.'

'You speak with such wisdom, but I wonder what you would say if you knew the truth.'

Emma stared up at him in abject silence for a moment. She had never heard such raw anguish in a man's voice before and, coming from Julien, it was all the more surprising. It touched her compassionate heart to ignite a warmth that swelled until it seemed to fill her being, and she was trembling with the force of it when she asked quietly, 'What is the truth?'

'I cannot tell you,' he said harshly, turning from her to fling his half-smoked cheroot into the sea, then he pushed his hands into his pockets and stood with his shoulders oddly hunched as he stared out across the shimmering ocean.

She wished that she could share his thoughts at that moment, for, whatever they were, she sensed that they were tearing him apart inside for some reason, and she saw the agony of it in the way he clenched his jaw until the muscles in his face jutted savagely.

It was in that instant that Emma realised she loved this man. It did not come as a shock to her, merely a quiet conviction which stole through her like a bright golden thread of emotion lassooing her heart, her mind, and her soul. She stepped forward on legs which seemed to move of their own volition, and she placed her hand lightly on his arm in an attempt to comfort him, but there was no slackening of the muscles beneath the expensive material of his impeccably tailored jacket.

'Julien?' she spoke his name for the first time without actually intending to, but it seemed to jar him back from whatever plane of thought he had travelled to.

He covered her comforting hand with one of his own, and turned slowly to face her. It seemed as if he wanted to say something, then he changed his mind and raised her hand to his lips. His mouth was warm against her cool palm, and the sensations that spiralled up the length of her arm sent little tremors racing through her which were wholly pleasurable. Their eyes met and held for interminable seconds, and the balmy silence of the night made the rapid beat of her heart sound like the heavy pounding of the *sega* drum. Could he hear it? she wondered crazily the one minute, and the next she was in his arms as if it was the most natural place on earth to be while his mouth found hers in the darkness.

She clung to him, drugged by his kisses and the wild emotions clamouring through her, and her softness yielded against him when his hands moved against her back to mould her into the hard curve of his body. His mouth left hers to trail a path of burning kisses along the sensitive cord of her neck down to her shoulder, but they returned again to plunder her lips like a man who had found water in the desert after thirsting for many days.

Intoxicated, Emma returned his kisses, her lips moving beneath his in a passionate response she could not withhold, and when at last they drew apart it was as if they both realised that this moment had to end, but he did not release her entirely. His hands were beneath her hair, framing her flushed face to raise it to his, and the tenderness in his touch made her want to weep for some ridiculous reason.

'I will not apologise for that, but it must not happen again.' Julien's voice was quiet, but determined as he thrust her back into the bewildering reality of a life outside the comforting strength of his arms. So many questions raced through her mind, but she could not seek the answers while her mind was still spinning away from that dangerous edge of desire, and her lips were still tingling in the aftermath of his kisses. 'Come,' instructed Julien, lowering his hands to take her arm. 'It is time to leave.'

Emma did not argue; she had neither the strength, nor the will to do so, but her mind was racing in ever increasing circles. Why, why, *why*? Why did he kiss her and then say it must never happen again? Was it because of Daniella Bertrand? Was he ashamed, perhaps, of seeking comfort in the arms of someone other than Daniella? Jealousy seared Emma like a flame, and she hated herself for it, but it also acted as a spur to pull herself together. She had been ashamed of herself before for inviting his kisses, but she felt no shame now. Julien had wanted her kisses as much as she had wanted his; she had felt it in the fast, heavy beat of his heart against her and, loving him as much as she did, she was crazy enough to believe that he was not totally indifferent to her.

In the well-lit restaurant Julien's remote expression told her nothing, and she could almost dislike him for looking so calm while everything within her still quivered with the memory of those magical moments in his arms.

'*Mon cher*, where have you been?' Daniella questioned anxiously when they reached their table. 'We have been quite concerned,' she added, a hint of venom in her dark eyes when she glanced at Emma.

'The breeze outside was more enjoyable than dancing in this heat,' Julien explained smoothly. 'I think we will all go to the villa for coffee before we retire for the night. Do you agree, Louis?'

'It is as you wish,' Louis bowed to his decision, but there was a query in his eyes when they met Emma's.

She realised that Louis was curious and perhaps a little annoyed, but she pretended an innocence which did not come easily at that moment while her lips still tingled slightly from the pressure of Julien's mouth.

Julien and Louis had a slight dispute about who would settle the bill, but Louis was no match for Julien in a dispute, and ten minutes later Emma was being driven back to the villa in Louis' car. This time, however, Julien's Bentley was following close behind them, and its headlights lit the interior of Louis' BMW.

'Is there something troubling you, Louis?' Emma spoke for the first time since leaving the hotel, and a rueful smile curved his mouth.

'If I am silent, *chérie*, it is because I am lamenting over an evening which has not turned out quite as I had hoped.'

'What, exactly, had you hoped for?' she laughed, amazed that her sense of humour was still intact.

'I had hoped that after dinner we could go for a quiet stroll on Belle Mare's lovely beach, and perhaps we could have ended the evening with a sociable drink at my home.'

A quiet stroll on the beach. Those words made her heart beat faster, but they also left a faintly bitter taste in her mouth.

'Where is your home?' she questioned him merely for the sake of shutting her mind temporarily to what had occurred.

'My home is a private suite in the hotel where we have dined this evening.'

'Oh,' she said, and she understood now why the chief steward had known Louis by name.

Louis glanced at her sharply. 'Why do you say "*oh*" so strangely?'

'I was wondering if you are still able to count the number of women who have seen the inside of your private hotel suite.'

'You have a wicked mind, *chérie*,' he laughed out loud at her bluntness.

'Can you deny the truth?' she challenged him.

'With anyone else but you I would have denied it most strongly, but you are much too clever for that, so I shall not insult your intelligence,' he admitted soberly. 'I have taken many women up to my suite, but with you my intentions were strictly honourable, and that, Emma, is the truth.'

'Do you know something?' she said after a momentary pause for thought. 'I believe you.'

'*Merci,*' he said, and his hand left the wheel briefly to squeeze hers. She felt herself relax slowly, but the next instant he shot a question at her that drove the tension straight back into her muscles. 'What happened when you were alone on the beach with Julien?'

'Nothing happened,' she almost snapped. 'We went out for a breath of fresh air, and we talked about Dominic.'

She thanked heaven that this was partly the truth, but the rest was no one's business but her own.

'I believe you,' Louis was saying, 'but I do not think that Daniella will feel the same as I do.'

'I don't particularly care what she believes,' Emma answered rashly.

'She has sharp claws, that kitten,' he warned mockingly. 'Take care, *chérie*, that she does not become your enemy.'

It was almost midnight when they arrived at the villa, but coffee had been left in a silver flask in the *salon*, and cups had been set out in a tray on the low table between the chairs. Daniella poured, taking on the task of hostess with a confidence which stung, and as a result Emma made no attempt to join in the conversation. Jealousy was something new to her, but she would have to learn to suppress it, for Daniella, it seemed, was in Julien's life to stay.

Louis did not linger after he had had his coffee, and Emma rose quickly to accompany him out to his car. There was something she needed to know, and she could not question him in front of Julien.

'Did you mean it when you said that Julien had despised his wife?' she asked Louis when he slid behind the wheel of his car and inserted the key in the ignition.

Emma saw his hands clench on the wheel, and he was

silent for such interminable seconds that she thought he was not going to answer her, then he said with a strange harshness in his usually suave voice, 'Do me a favour, *chérie*, and forget that I ever told you that. *Bonne nuit.*'

He turned the key in the ignition, and Emma stepped back when the engine roared to life, but her eyes were thoughtful when they followed his car out of the driveway.

He was hiding something, she was certain of that, and suddenly she was more determined than ever to delve more deeply into the mystery surrounding the death of Marguerite Perreau.

Emma said goodnight and went up to her room, but an hour later she was still awake when Julien took Daniella home. What was Louis hiding, and why had he said that Julien had despised his wife? Why was her name never mentioned, and why had her photographs been destroyed? There were so many questions that needed answering, and she wondered tiredly if she would ever know the complete truth.

She thought of those moments on the beach with Julien, and she absently fingered her lips. *I will not apologise for that, but it must not happen again*, Julien had said and, when she thought about it, it was the most confusing statement of all. He would not apologise for kissing her, but it must not happen again. If he would not apologise, then he had obviously *wanted* that moment of intimacy, but if it must not happen again, then *what* was the point? And *why* must it not happen again?

Questions spiralled and twisted through her mind until she drifted into an exhausted sleep, but even in her dreams they haunted her.

Emma had no way of knowing that soon the mystery would begin to unravel for her. Two days later, when she spent her free afternoon sunbathing on the beach, she became aware of something which instilled a distant fear in her. At first she could not place it, and she told herself that she was imagining things, but the next instant she knew what it was. It was the smell of garlic and curry, and she sat up abruptly to see a tall, middle-aged man standing no more than two paces away from her.

Fear brought the taste of ashes to her mouth as she grabbed her towelling robe and leapt to her feet. It took a moment to control herself sufficiently to speak, and she used that moment to thrust her arms into the sleeves of her robe in order to cover her bikini-clad figure.

'Who are you, and what do you want?' she finally demanded of the man with the lanky hair and dark, drooping moustache.

'I apologise for frightening you the other evening, but all I want is to talk to you,' he explained, his small, dark eyes observing her intently, and somewhat slyly while she fastened the belt about her waist.

'Well, *I* don't wish to talk to *you*,' she snapped, picking up her towel and turning to leave, but the next instant he said something that made her halt her actions abruptly.

'You would be wise to listen to what I have to say, Mademoiselle Gilbert.'

There was something sinister about the man, and it frightened her, but she hid her feelings admirably when she turned slowly to face him once again. 'How do you know my name?'

A row of broken teeth appeared between lips that parted in a smile which was more like a snarl. 'There is very little that happens on this part of the island that I do not know about.'

'I suggest you say what you have to say, and get it

over with,' she said coldly, impatient to get back to the safety of the villa.

'Evil lurks at the villa, *mademoiselle*,' he informed her, and there was a distinct threat in his voice. 'If you do not wish to become a part of that evil, then I suggest you return to your own country before it is too late.'

Too late for what? Emma wondered cynically. 'I don't frighten easily, you know, so you will have to be more explicit.'

'Very well,' he nodded, parting his lips in yet another snarl-like smile. 'Monsieur Perreau was on the patio with his wife on the very day she fell to her death.'

Incredulous anger swept through her. 'Are you perhaps insinuating that Monsieur Perreau pushed his wife down the steps?'

'I am not insinuating anything, *mademoiselle*, but he was seen on that day.'

'By whom?' she bit out the question, and that sinister snarl twisted his mouth once again.

'The source of my information I cannot disclose to you, but heed my warning, *mademoiselle*, or you may be the next to meet with an unfortunate accident.'

Emma was momentarily too shocked and stunned to speak and, by the time she had regained her voice, he had gone. How *dare* he accuse Julien of killing his wife! How dare he even suggest it! It was ridiculous! *Preposterous!* She would *never* believe it, and yet she was shaking like a leaf when she made her way back to the villa across the sand. The man had lied to her, but there had to be a reason for his lies. For some reason he wanted her away from the island and from Julien Perreau in particular. But for what reason? Julien had been seen out on the patio that fateful day two years ago when his wife had died. Seen by whom? And what was it that this mystery person had seen? Could he have seen Julien push his wife down the steps? *No!* Nothing on earth would ever make her believe Julien capable of such a monstrous act!

She found Celestine Perreau on the patio with her embroidery and, as usual, Nada was hovering dutifully in the background.

'*Madame*, may I have a private word with you before I go up and change?' Emma asked at once, and a look of surprise flashed across the older woman's lined face before she glanced at the young Indian girl.

'That will be all for now, Nada.'

'*Oui*, Madame Celestine,' the girl curtseyed slightly and disappeared into the house.

'What is troubling you, Emma?' asked Celestine anxiously when Emma pulled up a chair and sat down close to her. 'You are quite pale, *chérie*.'

'Something happened a little while ago; something rather unpleasant,' Emma confided in her, shuddering inwardly at the thought of what she had been told.

'You wish to talk about it?'

'Yes, *madame*.' Emma swallowed nervously, and clasped her hands tightly in her lap. '*Madame*, I don't wish to pry, but ... would you tell me how your daughter-in-law met her death?'

Celestine Perreau almost dropped her embroidery, but she caught it before it slipped off her lap, and she darted a nervous glance over her shoulder as if she expected someone might be standing behind her chair.

'That is not a subject which Julien wishes to have discussed in his home,' she rebuked Emma in a hushed voice, and there was a distinct look of fear in her eyes.

'I realise that, *madame*,' Emma assured her, lowering her voice to match the older woman's, 'but I was warned this afternoon that, if I did not leave the villa, I would become involved in the unsavoury repercussions of your daughter-in-law's death, and the one who warned me also tried to make me believe that your son was the cause of the accident.'

'*Nom de Dieu!* You did not believe this?'

This was the first time Emma had heard Celestine use such strong language and, when she met those shrewd, probing eyes, she shook her head emphatically. 'No, *madame*, I didn't believe it. I don't know your son very well, but I do know that he is much too honourable to even contemplate such a despicable deed.'

'He had a motive, Emma, and it was a very strong motive.'

Emma stared at her in horror. '*Madame* ... you surely don't believe ...'

'No, I cannot believe that my son would do anything which is so totally against his rigid beliefs,' Celestine interrupted Emma's halting query, and she gestured impatiently with her hands. 'Before I tell you more, may I know whom it was you spoke to?'

'The man was an Indian, and he reeked of garlic and curry. I asked his name, but he withheld it.'

'What did he look like?' Celestine questioned her closely, and Emma described him down to the last detail. 'Sammy Moodley. I should have guessed that it would be Sammy Moodley,' Celestine announced at length, and her expression looked grim.

'You know him?' asked Emma in surprise.

'Yes, I know him,' Celestine sighed tiredly. 'For eight years Sammy Moodley worked for Julien. First as paymaster on the plantation, then as a cashier at the hotel, but Julien discharged him when it was discovered that he was involved in illicit dealings with some of the patrons at the hotel, and ever since then Sammy has been indulging in petty little attempts to take revenge.'

'I see,' Emma murmured, parts of the puzzle beginning to fall into place, but there was still a great deal more she had to know.

'You were asking me about ... about Marguerite,' Celestine broached the subject before Emma could, and there was despair in her eyes. 'Their marriage was a mistake, and Julien suffered because of it. Marguerite made his life a misery from the very beginning, and I had to watch helplessly while my son died slowly inside during the five years of their marriage. She did not want children and, when she learned that she was pregnant with Dominic, she became totally unstable and tried several times to commit suicide. When Dominic was born she would not have him near her, and the child grew up very much in Nada's care and mine. Julien spent much of his time with Dominic, but after Marguerite's death ...'

Celestine paused and clutched at her throat. It was as if reliving the past was almost too much for her, and Emma did not press her to continue until Madame Celestine herself felt she was ready to do so, but a part of the villa's mystery was unravelling with remarkable clarity. If it was true that Julien had despised his wife, then Emma could now begin to understand why such feelings had been aroused in him.

CHAPTER SEVEN

THE silence on the patio was disturbed by an Indian myna when it flew down to perch with a noisy flutter of wings on the low wall surrounding the patio. These birds were a common sight along the east coast of South Africa, and Emma could still recall her initial surprise at finding mynas here in Mauritius. In captivity they could be taught to imitate the human voice almost to perfection, but Emma had always disliked the idea of curtailing a bird's freedom by keeping it imprisoned in a cage.

Celestine's chair creaked when she altered her position, and the Indian myna flew away, the white patch on its wings, and the white fringe around its tail clearly visible.

'I am afraid I do not know much about Marguerite's accident,' Madame Perreau continued where she had left off. 'I know only what Julien told me at that time, and that was not very much. It appears she fell down the flight of steps at the entrance to the villa, but Julien cannot recall the details leading directly up to the accident. It was Li who found Marguerite, and when he rushed inside to telephone for help, he found Julien lying unconscious on the patio with a wound on the side of his head. We still do not know if he fell and injured himself, or if he was struck by someone.'

'You mean his memory has blanketed out that entire incident?' asked Emma incredulously.

'That is what the doctors say,' Celestine nodded solemnly, her eyes staring blankly at something beyond Emma.

114

'And the police?' Emma prompted. 'I take it there was a police inquiry?'

'The police accepted the medical verdict, and agreed that the wound on Julien's head could not have been self-inflicted in order to mislead them.' Celestine sighed heavily and gestured helplessly with her hands. 'They have made it quite clear that they consider it was an unfortunate accident, but Julien cannot accept this while his memory continues to fail him. There is also the possibility that someone might have had some obscure reason to attack them both, but as yet the police have found no evidence of a third party being involved.'

Emma considered this for a moment, and she felt their uncertainty and their terrible anxiety as if it had become tangible like the towelling cloth of her beach robe. 'Do you suspect that Sammy Moodley might have had something to do with it?'

'Non.' Celestine was quite adamant. 'Sammy Moodley may be accused of many other crimes, but he is not capable of violence.'

Emma bit her lip and absently twisted the belt of her robe about her thumb. 'What do *you* think happened, *madame*?'

Celestine Perreau unnecessarily rearranged the embroidery in her lap, and the anguish in her dark eyes tore at Emma's heart and brought a lump to her throat.

'I have lain awake many nights thinking about it, but each thought has been more frightening than the one before,' she confided in a voice which was not quite steady. 'I do not want to think anymore, it is futile, but I do know that I have faith in my son.'

'And Julien?' Emma questioned in a hushed voice. 'What are his theories?'

'I do not know, and I dare not ask what he thinks,' Celestine confessed despairingly. 'His instructions were that Marguerite's name was never to be mentioned, and so also the subject of her death has never been discussed. My son, Emma, had become a stranger to me. I cannot understand what has changed him so, and there are times when I am actually afraid of him.'

'Oh, *madame* . . .' Momentarily too choked to speak, Emma crossed the space dividing them and knelt at Celestine Perreau's feet to take those slender, bejewelled hands between her own. 'Thank you for telling me all you know, and I give you my word that it shall go no further.'

A smile softened her thin-lipped features, and there was also a glimmer of relief in her eyes when she looked down at Emma. '*Merci, ma chérie*, and thank you for making me speak of these things. It has been inside me for so long that there have been times I could not distinguish between the facts, and my own terrible imagination.'

Emma leaned forward impulsively and kissed her perfumed cheek. 'I must go up and change, *madame*, and since I haven't gone out this afternoon I shall wake Dominic from his nap, and take care of him until it is time for his bath.'

Celestine nodded, a sudden glimmer of tears in her eyes, and Emma left her out there on the patio with her embroidery and her painful thoughts which only the truth could eradicate.

Emma's own mind was a mad whirl of thoughts. Was it possible that Julien feared he might have participated in some way to cause the death of his wife? She tried to put herself in his position, and the result was quite devastating.

As the days passed, and her second month at the villa drew to a close, Emma found herself thinking almost of nothing else but the conversation she had had with Celestine Perreau. There had to be some way to help

Julien, but if nothing had been achieved in the two
years since Marguerite's death, then what could she do
which had not been done already.

She was pondering this question again one afternoon
when, instead of resting after lunch, she went for a walk
in the garden. There had to be *something* she could do
to help Julien, she was thinking as she approached the
edge of the Perreau property, but the next instant her
thoughts were scattered when she heard a sound above
her in the trees. She glanced up to see a young, dark-
skinned Indian boy of about twelve sitting in the fork of
a tree, and he was perched so high that Emma felt her
neck aching just to have to look up at him.

'What are you doing up there?' she questioned him
after a startled silence had prevailed.

'I climb trees,' he answered her in broken, heavily
accented English.

'That much is obvious,' she smiled wryly. 'I suppose
you know that you're on Perreau property?'

'I know,' he surprised her with his truthfulness. 'Big
trees only here for climbing.'

'You come here often?' she asked incredulously.

'Sometimes,' came the cautious reply.

'Look here, don't you think you could climb down
now?' Emma fingered her neck at the base of her skull.
'It's awfully difficult trying to talk to you while my neck
is almost cracking with the effort to see you.'

A shadow of fear flashed across his face for the first
time. 'If I climb down you will take me to Monsieur
Perreau, and he will beat me.'

'Why would I take you to Monsieur Perreau, and
why would he want beat you?' she questioned him in
shocked surprise.

'My father say he will.'

'That's rubbish!' she contradicted with some annoyance. 'Anyway, Monsieur Perreau isn't here at the

moment, and he won't be here until late this afternoon.'

The young boy still hesitated. 'You sure?'

'Of course I'm sure,' she replied emphatically. 'Now climb down, will you, or I'm going to have a permanent crick in my neck.'

There was still a momentary hesitation, then he climbed down with the agility of a monkey, and dropped down to the ground in front of her.

'That's better,' she smiled down at him, and her smile dashed away that final little flicker of fear she had noticed in his eyes as he studied her intently.

'You pretty.'

'I beg your pardon?' she asked, startled by the unexpectedness of his remark.

'My father say you pretty, so I come see, and . . . you pretty.'

'Thanks for the compliment,' she murmured, but her mind was suddenly alert to something else. 'What's your name?'

'Reggie Moodley, *mademoiselle*.'

'Oh!' She had more or less guessed, but it still came as a shock, and she only barely succeeded in hiding her feelings. 'Where do you stay?'

'We stay on plantation not far from here,' he said, pointing in the general direction of Curepipe.

'I see.'

'You tell Monsieur Perreau about me?' The fear was back in his eyes, and he was instantly poised for flight. 'You tell him I climb tree?'

'I shan't tell him anything, so you can stop behaving like a scared rabbit,' she announced calmly.

'I got rabbit at home,' he smiled for the first time, 'and they going to have babies soon.'

'How nice,' she murmured absently, her mind leaping about like a wild plantation monkey caught in a cage.

'You want baby rabbit?'

'No, thank you,' she declined hastily. 'I don't have anywhere to keep it.'

She could just imagine Julien Perreau's reaction if she should introduce a rabbit into the household, and the mere thought of his displeasure was enough to make her shrink inwardly.

'My father say you must leave the island.'

Emma glanced at the young boy sharply. 'Did he send you here to tell me that?'

'Non,' Reggie shook his head. 'I hear him talk when he think I am asleep.'

'You heard him saying that I must leave the island?' she sought confirmation of Reggie's statement while her mind leapt from one thought to the next.

'Oui,' he nodded.

'Do you know why?'

'He say you meddle in things that are not your business.'

'I see.' The mystery was beginning to unravel a little more. Sammy was afraid she might discover something. But what? 'Does your father know that you heard him talking?'

'Oh, non!' he exclaimed in a hushed voice, his dark eyes widening until they were almost like saucers in his face.

'You're afraid of your father?' she asked, recalling her own fear when she had met Sammy Moodley.

'He will beat me if he know I speak to you.'

He spoke with such conviction that she believed him, but something forced her to question him more closely. 'Why would he beat you if he found out you have spoken to me?'

'My father say I must not speak to anyone here at the villa,' came the reply, and he was too young to disguise the fear in his eyes.

'Why not?' Emma persisted, and he darted a nervous glance about him before he hung his head and kicked at a pebble close to his bare toes.

'I not speak to anyone.'

A thought leapt unbidden into her mind, and it was filled with such alarming possibilities that she shivered inwardly with a mixture of fear and excitement. She stared down at Reggie's bent head, and very casually she asked: 'Do you like climbing trees?'

'Oui,' he nodded, looking up and gesturing with his arms. 'If I climb trees I can see very far.'

'That's true,' Emma agreed, controlling that surge of incredible hope and excitement as she glanced up into the tree where she had found Reggie, then she lowered her gaze to his again. 'You said you come here often to climb trees.'

His mouth drooped and that flicker of fear was back again in his dark eyes. 'Not so much now.'

'But once you used to come here often?' she continued to question him while her mind went wild with the one thought which kept circulating through it.

'Oui,' Reggie muttered. 'But now my father forbid it.'

'Your father doesn't like Monsieur Perreau, does he,' she risked voicing the obvious, and the young boy's face became sullen and guarded.

'I must go,' he announced, preparing for flight.

'Reggie?' she stopped him with a firm hand on his shoulder, and he glanced up at her warily. 'I won't tell anyone that you were here, and I won't tell either if you want to come again.'

She could feel the tension in his shoulder muscles, and he took such a long time to answer her that she found herself holding her breath for some reason.

'Maybe I come again,' he said at length, shrugging off her hand. *'Sallam.'*

'Sallam, Reggie,' she responded to his Creole

greeting, and she stood there watching him while he climbed over the low stone wall.

He darted a glance at her, and then he was gone, but Emma stood there for some time with her mind in a crazy turmoil. Was it possible? Or was she simply grasping at anything that seemed remotely like a miracle? There was only one way to find out and, glancing down at her cool linen slacks, she decided that it was time for action.

Taking off her leather-soled sandals, she pulled herself up on to the lowest branch of the tree, and then she began the arduous climb up to where she had seen Reggie perching. It was years since she had done anything quite as crazy as this, and she hated the thought of what might be said if someone should find her there, but there was something she had to find out for herself, and the only way she could do so was by climbing that particular tree. The bark was rough beneath the soft pads of her feet, and she had developed a fear of heights over the years which sent a wave of giddy nausea surging through her, but she gritted her teeth and continued her climb.

An Indian myna screeched almost indignantly on a branch above her, very nearly making her lose her foothold, but she clung desperately to the base of the tree, and doggedly continued her climb until she could ease herself wearily on to the fork in the tree where Reggie had sat. She was panting from the unaccustomed exertion, but it was nothing compared to the way she felt when she glanced in the direction of the villa. She had a clear view of the patio and the steps down which Marguerite Perreau had supposedly fallen to her death. Emma shuddered involuntarily. She had walked up and down those steps so often during the past two months, but she had never once given a thought to the tragedy which had occurred there. Did Julien think about it often? Is that why she saw him so often, late at night, smoking a cheroot on the patio, and staring down those steps into the garden? Was he trying to prod his memory in the hope that it would unveil the truth which was still kept hidden from him?

She felt tears pricking her eyelids, and she swallowed convulsively at the lump in her throat. *Julien!* her heart cried out his name in despair when she thought of how distant he had become since that night he had kissed her on the beach. She thrust aside her painful thoughts and stared instead at the patio with the steps leading down into the colourful garden, and her mind ran riot as she mentally ticked off the facts. Reggie was afraid of his father. He had always climbed the trees at the villa, but now he had been forbidden to do so. He had also been forbidden to talk to anyone, especially someone at the villa. Why? Was Reggie simply afraid of his father, or was there something else which frightened him? Something he had seen two years ago, perhaps?

Emma climbed down gingerly, her heart in her mouth most of the time, and she breathed a sigh of intense relief when she finally lowered herself to the ground. The soles of her feet felt a little raw when she slipped on her sandals, and so did her hands, but her mind was too busy with what she had discovered. It was possible that Reggie Moodley could have been perched in that tree on the very evening Marguerite Perreau had died. It was also possible that he had seen everything, but for some diabolical reason his father had forbidden him to speak of it. If this was so, then Reggie possessed the key to the final mystery. Emma knew that she was perhaps fantasising, but the possibility could not be overlooked, and she could only hope that Reggie would make an effort to see her again. If she could gain his confidence, then she might succeed in learning the truth, and Julien may then at last have his peace of mind restored. Or would the truth be of such a nature that it would have quite the opposite effect? Emma did not even want to think about the latter.

Julien did not have dinner with them that evening. Celestine announced that he was at a conference for hoteliers, and that he would arrive home late. Emma could not decide whether she was relieved, or disappointed. Either way, it would not have mattered. Julien had stoically ignored her since that evening they had dined at the Belle Mare hotel. He had acknowledged her existence with a curt nod each time, but other than that she had not existed for him, and his aloofness on this occasion hurt her more than anything else had ever done before.

Celestine retired early, but Emma remained out on the patio for some time after she had gone. She stared at the steps, and tried to imagine what had occurred there two years ago to send Marguerite hurtling down to her death on the paved driveway below. Emma shuddered, but she could not turn her mind away from the thought. What did Marguerite look like? Was she beautiful? Had Julien loved her very much once?

She sighed audibly and went inside. There was no need to lock the doors, for Li was like an ever present watchdog in the grounds at night, and she sometimes wondered if he ever took time off to sleep.

She went to bed, but she lay staring into the darkness with her mind leaping from one thing to the other. She thought about Reggie, and she wondered if her suspicions would ever be confirmed. Sammy had told her that day on the beach that Julien had been seen out on the patio with his wife on the day she had died. He would not give her the name of his informant, and this of course made it possible that it could have been Reggie. Reggie could have witnessed something which might have cleared Julien completely, but Sammy, wanting to avenge himself on Julien, would naturally force his son to remain silent. It was logical, but it was also a terrible way to take revenge, and she wondered again whether she would ever manage to get the truth out of Reggie . . . if indeed he knew the truth.

Emma sat up with a sigh and glanced at the luminous hands of her bedside clock. It was almost midnight, but her mind was too active to give her any peace. She swung her legs off the bed and pushed her feet into her soft mules while she slipped her arms into the sleeves of her silk robe. The moon was casting a pale light across the floor, making it easy for her to see where she was going as she walked into her small lounge, and she snapped on the reading lamp before selecting a book from the shelf against the wall. Reading had always helped her to relax in the past, but she was sitting curled up in her chair an hour later, and staring blankly at the open book in her lap. She had not read one word and, if she had, then nothing had penetrated the barrier of her stormy thoughts.

You're crazy! That was what Lucy had said, and Emma was certainly beginning to think that she had been right. Two months ago she had not been aware that Julien Perreau existed, and now she was suddenly up to her ears in the intrigue which surrounded him. She had become inordinately fond of Dominic and, worst of all, she had been foolish enough to fall in love with her employer. Lucy would be horrified if she knew this. She had accused Emma of being fussy, and that is exactly what Emma had been where men were concerned, but in no time at all she had lost her heart to a man like Julien Perreau. He was autocratic, arrogant, ruthless, and savage at times, but she had also come to know the gentle, caring, and passionate side of him. He was a complex man, with many moods, and to top it all he was living under the shadow of his wife's death.

Of all the nice, easy-going men she could have chosen from, Emma had been unwise enough to give her heart to a man like Julien, and at that precise moment she could foresee nothing but heartache ahead of her. He could never care for her, not as she cared for him, and then there was Daniella Bertrand. Daniella was beautiful and intelligent, and above all they seemed to suit each other so well that Emma was overcome with misery at the mere thought of it.

Emma could not entirely understand Julien. Twice he had kissed her with a tender, but driving passion, and on both occasions he had finally thrust her aside as if he had committed an unforgivable crime. First he had said that he had had no right to kiss her, and the other night at the Belle Mare hotel he had said: 'I will not apologise for that, but it must not happen again.' Had he simply been amusing himself with her, or had she unknowingly led him on to believe that she was eager for his kisses?

She cringed inwardly at the thought. She could not deny that, in a strange fit of madness, she had invited his kisses that night of the cyclone, but she could not recall doing so on the beach at Belle Mare. It may have seemed so to Julien, and if he was committed to Daniella Bertand, then it was no wonder he had said that it must not happen again. Oh, God! How was she going to live through the next ten months loving him as much as she did, and knowing that he could never care for her? She did not even want to think about all those empty years which would surely follow.

'You're too fussy,' she recalled her sister's words, and Emma admitted to herself that it was true. There would be other men, she supposed, but there could never be another Julien Perreau. To Emma he was unique; he was that someone special she had always hoped to meet, and she knew that no other man could ever make her feel the way she had felt when Julien had held her in his arms. He had shown her a little glimpse of heaven and, knowing herself, she would never be satisfied with anything else.

Her eyes filled with tears. She tried to blink them back, but they spilled from her lashes and rolled down her cheeks. She put the book aside and tried desperately to control herself, but the hot tears continued to flow until she put her head down on her arms and wept in a way she had not done for years. Her bout of weeping left her feeling drained, but she knew that she would not sleep if she went to bed, so she dried her eyes and blew her nose, and simply sat there quietly while the hands of the clock shifted on to one-thirty in the morning.

She was lost in thought again, and she was so busy piecing together the bits of information she had received that she never heard the lounge door being opened. Julien featured so strongly in her mind that the sound of his deep, velvety voice seemed to merge with her thoughts, but almost simultaneously she was startled by the realisation that he was actually in the room with her.

'Emma?' Her name came from him in a soft query, and she leapt to her feet, clutching her blue robe about her slender body, and fastening the belt with hands that shook as she stood facing him.

'Monsieur . . .' She tried to say something more, but she could not, and she simply stood there staring at him.

He was not wearing his jacket, and his white shirt had been unbuttoned almost to the waist to reveal the silver crucifix which he always wore on a chain about his sun-browned throat. At that time of night, and after days of being practically ignored, it seemed to her that never before had she been confronted by such raw masculinity. She felt herself begin to tremble with an awareness of her own femininity, and her insides instantly coiled themselves into one mass of aching longing.

'I saw your light on when I arrived,' he said, his glance holding hers as he closed the door and walked towards her. 'It is very late.'

'I know,' she murmured huskily, lowering her lashes to veil her eyes, and intensely conscious of the fact that she was wearing only a flimsy nighty beneath an equally flimsy robe. Her hair was a tousled mess, and her face was devoid of make-up, but worst of all was the uncontrollable hammering of her heart which she felt certain he could hear.

'You are not well?' he asked, the expensive leather of his shoes coming into her line of vision.

'I am—quite well, thank you,' she managed, her throat almost too tight to speak.

'Look at me, Emma.' It was a command even though it was quietly spoken, and she could not disobey him. His dark, narrowed eyes searched her raised face, and his mouth tightened. 'You have been crying.'

She was overcome suddenly with a surge of longing to resume her bout of weeping in his arms, and the fear that she might actually do so made her turn from him abruptly. 'I haven't been crying, I——'

'I am not blind, *mademoiselle*,' he interrupted her curtly and with a hint of anger in his voice. 'I did try to warn you about Louis, and I attempted to protect you with my presence the other night at Belle Mare, but it seems I have failed.'

Julien imagined she had been crying because of Louis! The thought of it was so incredible it made her want to laugh, but it also angered her that he could have presumed she would be idiot enough to be taken in by a man like Louis Villet.

'I don't need your protection, *monsieur*.'

'No?' he demanded with that icy sarcasm which came so easily to him. 'Then may I know why you were sitting here, at this time of the morning, with the trace of recent tears in your eyes?'

Oh, God, help me! she thought, but aloud she said: 'That is my business, *monsieur*.'

'Emma!' His voice rebuked her sharply, but his hands on her shoulders were warm and strangely gentle when he turned her to face him. 'I do not want to see you hurt. *Mon Dieu*, do you think I do not know Louis Villet? There have been so many women, and when he has done with them they are of as little use to him as an old pair of shoes.'

Her senses were stirred by the mixture of tobacco and masculine cologne which clung to him, but she forcibly shut her mind to it. 'I know exactly what kind of man Louis is.'

'You know?' His eyebrows rose a fraction. 'And yet you have let matters go this far?'

At any other time she might have found a snappy answer with which to evade his query, but the gentle warmth of his hands on her shoulders was draining her anger from her, and she was left with only the truth. 'I was not crying because of Louis.'

Julien's eyes narrowed to dark slits as they probed hers. 'You were not, you say?'

'No,' she shook her head and lowered it so that her hair fell forward to veil her expression.

'Emma?' His hands left her shoulders to slide beneath her hair until they framed her face, and an unbearable tension spiralled between them when he forced her to meet his burning gaze. Her heart was beating in her throat, and she could feel her cheeks flaming with embarrassment against his palms. 'I am the one who has made you weep?' Julien questioned her with a look of incredulity in his eyes.

'Oh, please!' she begged in a choked voice, her hands going up to his wrists in an attempt to free herself, but his fingers had become locked in the tangled golden mass of her hair, and her hands fell away from his strong wrists to hang limply at her sides.

'*Chérie,*' he murmured the endearment in that velvety voice which was so like a caress, and every nerve in her body seemed to respond to it in a delirious fashion. 'I am not worthy of your tears.'

Everything within her stilled suddenly as if she were holding her breath for endless seconds, and the grimness of his expression sent a flicker of fear darting through her. 'Why—Why do you say that?'

'I say it because it is the truth,' he sighed, releasing her abruptly and moving away from her as if he could no longer bear to be near her.

'What is the truth?'

The ensuing silence in the room was deafening. Had she gone too far? Was she probing too deeply into something which, technically speaking, did not concern her?

'You have asked me that before, and once again I must say that I cannot tell you,' Julien answered her at length, his formidable back turned rigidly towards her, but this time she would not be shut out.

'*Why* can't you tell me?' she risked pursuing the subject.

'I cannot tell you because I do not know the truth myself,' he replied harshly, his hands clenching at his sides. '*Mon Dieu,* I wish I did!'

'Julien . . .' she pleaded hesitantly. 'You can't spend the rest of your life shutting out the past.'

'What do you know about the past?' he rounded on her so savagely that she backed a pace away from him.

'I know your wife died two years ago when she fell down the steps at the entrance to the villa,' she replied, knowing that only the truth would suffice.

'Who told you that?' he shot the question at her angrily, and she was thankful that she had an explanation ready which would not involve anyone close to him.

'I was sitting next to a businessman on the plane coming out here. He obviously spends a lot of time in Mauritius and, when I mentioned your name, he told me about your wife.'

The muscles seemed to jut out along the side of Julien's jaw when he swung away from her. 'I do not wish to discuss it.'

'Why not?' her blunt query stopped him before he reached the door, and he shot an angry glance at her over his shoulder.

'It is a subject which I have forgotten.'

'I never imagined that you were a coward, Monsieur Perreau.'

The air seemed to crackle at once with electricity, and Emma stood there feeling amazed at herself and also a little afraid. *This* time she had gone too far. It was one thing to question him, but it was quite a different matter to accuse him bluntly of being a coward, and she could see the fury in every line of his striking features.

'A coward?' he demanded in a clipped voice, crossing the room to tower over her, and it was only with the greatest difficulty that she withstood the ferocity of his glance. 'You think I am a coward?'

There was no turning back now. She had set the pace, and she had to keep to it. 'Why have you never made any attempt to search for the truth?'

'The truth!' he snarled, the veins standing out on his forehead, and his right fist slammed into the palm of his left hand with a loud cracking sound that made her jump visibly with fright. 'I would give my soul to know the truth!' he continued harshly. 'I have sat and thought about it until my head pounds, but the truth is locked away in my mind, and sometimes I think it is driving me insane!'

She felt his agony as if it were her own, and she desperately wanted to help him. 'Tell me about it?'

She sensed the tension gripping every muscle in his tall, lean body, and she saw it in the tightness of his features. He was resisting her quietly spoken suggestion that he should unburden himself to her and, for a moment, she thought he was going to reject her offer, then his shoulders sagged, and he brushed his hand over his eyes in a gesture of defeat that made her heart ache for him.

'I need a cognac,' he grunted tiredly, and she took him by the arms to propel him towards the door as if he had no will of his own to move.

'Go downstairs and pour yourself a cognac while I put some clothes on, and I'll meet you in your study in a few minutes.'

Emma was surprised at her own temerity to take command of him in this manner, but she was even more surprised at the way he willingly and silently agreed to her suggestion. When he had left she darted quickly into her bedroom and changed into slacks and a thin sweater. She brushed the tangles out of her hair and, with her mules still on her feet, she left her suite quietly and went downstairs to join Julien Perreau in his study.

CHAPTER EIGHT

THE glass doors leading out on to the patio had been opened wide, and the warm, scented night air filtered into the study. Julien stood framed in the doorway with a glass of cognac in his hand, and he did not turn from his intense study of the darkened garden when Emma entered the room from the direction of the hall. He was aware of her presence, she could see it in the way his shoulders moved slightly beneath the silk of his shirt and, when she reached his side, his dark eyes met hers briefly before he swallowed down the last of his cognac.

He poured himself another from the bottle which stood conveniently on the table behind him, and the dim light of the reading lamp accentuated the grimness of his expression, giving his lean face a harsh, haunted look. Emma loved him then with a fierceness that made her wish that she could ease his pain, but she did not have the right, and neither did she dare reveal her feelings for him so completely. Their glances met and she sensed the resistance in him, but they both knew that there were certain facts he could no longer withhold from her.

'I have not talked about ... about Marguerite for almost two years,' he said finally in a voice that sounded heavy with the burden of his thoughts as he stood staring down into the glass of cognac he held in his hand, then a cynical smile twisted his mouth. 'I was besotted with her when I met her seven years ago, but we were married less than a year when I discovered she was a devil, not a woman. In our faith we do not believe in divorce, so I knew that I would have to make the best of what was left of my marriage. Marguerite had made it quite clear that she never wanted children, but I imagined she would feel differently about it in time. I was wrong. When she discovered that she was pregnant she—she became like one possessed by a demon. She tried to kill herself twice and, for almost nine months, I had to guard her night and day with the assistance of Li. When Dominic was born she would not have him near her, and between *Maman*, Nada, and myself we cared for him while Marguerite continued her wild existence. *Mon Dieu!*' He swallowed down his drink in one gulp and thumped the glass down on to the table to light a cheroot. 'Our marriage was over ... *finished*, and all I felt for her was disgust when she paraded her lovers in front of me as another woman might parade the clothes she has bought.'

'Oh, Julien,' Emma breathed, her love reaching out to him, but he was unaware of it as he let the anguish flow from him.

'I cannot remember what happened on the day she died,' he continued as if Emma had not spoken. 'I know I came home that afternoon to find that Marguerite was out, but this was not unusual. I poured myself a cognac, and I can recall drinking it out there on the patio. Two hours later I was lying on my bed with the doctor and Li standing beside me. I am told that Li found me unconscious on the patio with a wound on the side of my head, but I do not know why, or how I could have hurt myself.' He drew hard on his cheroot and exhaled the smoke forcibly as if it helped in some way to rid him of his anger and his frustration. 'They say it was an accident, but I cannot accept that. *Le bon Dieu* knows that I despised Marguerite enough to want to kill her many times. Every man has his limits and, when I think about it, it is quite possible that she may have infuriated me that day to the extent that I——'

'*No!*' Emma went to him then, her hands gripping his arms, and through his shirt she could feel the taut muscles rippling beneath her fingers. 'I will never believe that. *Never!*'

'It is possible,' he insisted, looking down into her upturned face with dark, haunted eyes, but she shook her head adamantly.

'No, it is not, and you must stop thinking such thoughts.'

'Emma!' Her name passed his lips with a mixture of anguish and exasperation. He broke free of her touch, and turned from her to crush his cheroot in the ashtray. 'You do not know how very much I longed to be free of Marguerite, and in all truth I must confess that I often came close to wishing her dead,' he confided, leaning with his hands on his desk.

A coldness shifted through her veins, but her understanding and her faith in him triumphed. 'Wishing someone dead and actually killing them are two totally different things, and you're letting guilt destroy you because circumstances, at times, made you harbour the desire for freedom.'

He straightened to press his fingers against his temples as if they ached, then he dropped his hands and turned towards her with a look of resignation on his face which ripped at her soul.

'Yes, I do feel guilty. Marguerite wanted her freedom, and so did I. Perhaps if I had agreed to a divorce she would have been alive today, but instead I refused because of my faith.'

Emma shook her head and the tender warmth in her eyes matched the smile that curved her lips. 'You can't build your future on futile speculations.'

'You think that?' he asked, his features etched harshly in the dim light. 'You think I can be happy with the knowledge that I may have driven Marguerite to her death?'

'I think that ... for Dominic's sake ... you should attempt to live a life with some semblance of normality,' she whispered, her eyes not wavering from his.

Julien would have to tread a lonely path to overcome his feelings of guilt. Much as she wanted to, she knew she could not help him, and her eyes stung with tears. If those missing hours in his memory were restored to him it might ease his burden, and she was more determined than ever now to discover the truth.

She looked up into his smouldering eyes, and for a breathless eternity she had the strangest feeling that they were being united spiritually. The vibrations flowed between them like a strong current to culminate in a near electrical fusion of their minds, and she trembled with the force of it while she lost herself in his dark, compelling eyes. They were drawn together until she was locked in his arms, and he strained her softness to him with a fierceness that crushed her breasts against the hard wall of his chest.

'Emma ... Emma ...' he murmured thickly into her fragrant hair, then his lips sought hers, and she was lost in the tumultuous tide of her own emotions as the white-hot passion of his kisses seared her to her soul. It felt as if she was drowning, and she clung to his shoulders for safe anchorage in this wild storm that raged inside of her.

With his mouth on hers, he lifted her in his arms and carried her towards the sofa. She felt the softness of the cushions beneath her, and he followed her down to hold her there with the weight of his body as if he were afraid that she might attempt to escape him.

A breath of sanity invaded her drugged mind, warning that this situation was not without an element of danger, but his hard thighs were moving against her own, and his hands were beneath her thin sweater, his fingers caressing her waist and the sensitive hollow in her back. There was fire in his touch, and it inflamed her with sensations that sent an intoxicating languour into her limbs. His mouth moved against hers, exploring the sweetness within, and demanding a response which she did not withhold.

She loved him. Oh, God, how she loved him. Nothing else mattered beyond that, and she welcomed the touch of his hands against her breasts as if she had actually longed for it. His probing, caressing fingers aroused her to the point of pain and, when he finally pushed up her sweater to seek the swollen peak of her breasts with his mouth, a shudder of desire rippled through her. His mouth was hot and moist, his lips and his tongue teasing her nipples into hard buttons of aching desire, and a moan of intense pleasure spilled from her parted lips.

A deep-seated longing rose within her, a longing to be closer still to this man she loved, and her hands found their way into his shirt to explore his hair-roughened chest and the smooth skin across his shoulders where the muscles were bunched into knots that rippled beneath her fingertips.

Emma felt his body grow taut against her, and the thrust of his hips made her realise that his need was as strong as her own. With someone else this knowledge might have frightened her, but with Julien it was so right and, when his mouth found hers again, she responded with a passion she had not known she possessed. His skin was damp beneath her palms, and the smell of tobacco and cognac on his breath mingled with the clean male smell of him. It quivered in her nostrils, as potent as a drug, and it heightened her arousal to a peak where she could no longer think beyond the throbbing, aching desire that pulsated through her.

Withdrawal was the farthest thing from her mind, and she was left to wonder afterwards what would have happened if Julien had not curbed his desire for her at that moment. He pushed himself away from her with a groan on his lips, and pulled her up on to her feet with him, but Emma was not ready for this swift downward plunge into reality. She had been too high on that dizzy cloud of ecstasy where he had taken her, and her body was still quivering with a need so intense that she wanted to cry out with the agony of it.

'You must go up to your room,' Julien was saying in a voice that sounded strangely hoarse while he steadied her swaying body. 'It is almost three o'clock in the morning.'

Confused and bewildered, she stared up into his face, and his rigid, shuttered expression shocked her back to sanity as nothing else could have done. She stepped away from him, feeling guilty and deprived at the same time, but mostly she felt ashamed. God knows, she had no reason to feel ashamed, but, when she searched his face and found no sign of emotion there, she wondered whether she had imagined that he had felt something for her simply because she had so desperately wanted him to.

'Julien . . .'

She raised her hands imploringly, but he turned away from her as if the sight of her repulsed him. 'Go . . . leave me!'

There was rejection in his harsh voice, and it cut her to the quick. For one frozen second she could not move, then she turned and fled from him, and when she reached the privacy of her suite she wished that she could go on running. Activity had eased the pain, but without it she felt the slow torture of a knife being driven into her soul, and she flung herself across her bed to burst into tears for the second time that night.

Emma sometimes marvelled at how she had managed to survive during the next few days, but she also knew that if it had not been for Dominic's cheerful, adorable nature, she might have wallowed foolishly in a well of self-inflicted misery. If Julien could behave as if nothing had happened, then so could she, and her determination had the effect of a blessedly strong antidote.

'Emma, you are not listening.'

'I'm sorry, Dominic,' she tried to laugh away her distracted behaviour, and at the same time she thrust Julien from her mind. 'What were you saying?' she asked, looking down into Dominic's tawny eyes.

'There was a boy up in that tree over there,' he said, pointing, and Emma directed a searching glance towards the outskirts of the garden, but she could see no one.

'Are you sure?' she questioned Dominic, her heart bouncing, and he nodded emphatically.

'I saw him.'

'He's gone now,' she remarked disappointedly, realising that it could only have been Reggie Moodley.

'He went away when he saw me looking,' Dominic informed her in his much improved English and, when he frowned, he looked so much like Julien that she hugged him impulsively in a rush of affection which she could not control.

'I'm sure he meant no harm up there in the tree,' she brushed aside the matter. 'Perhaps he was merely admiring this lovely garden.'

Dominic accepted her explanation with childish faith and, when they went inside a few minutes later, Emma wondered whether Reggie would come back again, but she did not have another opportunity that day to go alone into the garden.

It was in Curepipe that Emma met Louis Villet again.

She had spent her free afternoon buying the few things she needed, and she was returning to where Li awaited her in the Bentley when she saw Louis crossing the street towards her.

'Have you been following me again?' she questioned him suspiciously when he reached her side, and he laughed humorously.

'Not this time, *chérie*,' he assured her. 'I came up from Port Louis on business, but I am delighted that I should meet you here.'

'I'm on my way to meet Li,' she explained as he fell into step beside her.

'Ah, the faithful Li,' he murmured in a distinctly mocking manner which made her glance at him curiously, but his handsome face wore a bland expression which gave nothing away. 'Will you have dinner with me this evening at my hotel?'

Surprise held her silent for a moment, then she asked caustically, 'This is rather unexpected, isn't it?'

'The unexpected is always exciting, is it not?'

'Not always,' she replied, disliking his arrogant suaveness.

'Are you going to refuse me?'

'There's Li,' said Emma, ignoring his query and quickening her pace as she approached the Bentley parked close to the Royal College. 'And I am expected at the villa for dinner,' she added at length.

'That is a problem very easily solved, *chérie*,' Louis insisted when they reached the car and, as Li got out smartly to open the rear door, Louis took Emma's parcels from her and thrust them into Li's arms. 'You will take Mademoiselle Gilbert's parcels to the villa, Li, and you will inform Madame Celestine that *mademoiselle* is dining with me. Now, be off with you.'

'Just a minute,' Emma rounded on Louis when she saw a justifiable look of annoyance flash across Li's face. 'Since my arrival here in Mauritius Li has very kindly taken me wherever I have wanted to be, and I will not have you speaking to him as if he were a servant at your beck and call, or mine for that matter.'

Li seemed to grow several dignified inches while Louis stared at Emma almost in open-mouthed astonishment. Louis Villet had deserved to be taken down a peg or two, and Emma did not regret what she had done.

'*Pardonnez-moi*, Li,' he said eventually, but Emma could not be certain that he had meant it.

Li bowed slightly in acceptance of Louis' apology, but he ignored him completely the next instant as he turned to face Emma. 'I will take your parcels to the villa, *mademoiselle*, and I shall inform Madame Celestine that you will be dining out.'

'Thank you, Li,' she smiled at him warmly. 'You are very kind.'

Li returned that smile, and he bowed deeply before depositing her parcels on the back seat of the Bentley and driving away.

'I must admit, *chérie*, that I feared for a moment you would be too angry to dine with me this evening,' Louis confessed some minutes later when she was seated beside him in his car and was being driven towards Belle Mare.

'I *am* angry with you,' she admitted, 'but there does happen to be something of importance I wish to discuss with you.'

'Something of importance?' He darted a frowning glance at her. 'May I know the nature of this matter?'

'It can wait.'

His frown deepened. 'Now you have made me curious.'

'You will have to remain curious for a while longer, Louis,' she insisted calmly. 'What I want to discuss with you can't be discussed now while you are driving.'

'It is as serious as that?'

'It's *very* serious.'

Anything concerning Julien's peace of mind *was* serious, and her unexpected meeting with Louis made her realise that there were certain things only he could tell her. His odd behaviour the last time she had seen him had made her realise that he knew more than he was willing to talk about, but this time she had the leverage to make him tell her what she wanted to know.

Bathed in the red glow of the setting sun, the hotel at Belle Mare looked no less exotic than it had looked that night with its flickering lights and surrounded by a shimmering, luminous sea.

Louis took her arm when they entered the impressive foyer, but, instead of walking towards the arched passageway which led to the restaurant, he ushered her towards the stairs.

'Where are we going?' Emma questioned him.

'I am taking you up to my suite,' he announced, his hand tightening on her arm as they walked up the curved steps. 'We will have something to drink, and then I shall order a dinner for two to be sent up.'

She hung back hesitantly. 'I thought we would be dining in the restaurant.'

'If you have something so very serious to discuss with me, then perhaps my suite would be the best place to dine,' he explained, his smile mocking when he looked down into her dubious eyes. 'It will give us privacy for this discussion, will it not?'

Emma considered this for a moment, then she nodded resignedly. 'Perhaps you are right.'

The lounge in Louis' private suite was attractively furnished with wicker chairs and tables, and the cushions were a mixture of vivid red, pale yellow, and emerald green.

'Relax, Emma,' Louis instructed when she perched

tensely on the edge of a chair. 'My reason for inviting you to dine with me was for the need of your intelligent company, and not for your delightful body.'

Emma smiled humorously, not quite sure whether he expected her to feel flattered, or shattered. 'Have you lived here long?'

'*Non,*' he said, standing with his back to her while he poured a glass of wine for her and something stronger for himself. 'I have lived here for almost two years, but before that I had a little villa farther south from here.'

'What made you give up your villa for a home which isn't your own?'

He shrugged as he handed her her glass of wine. 'There was no longer any reason to keep the villa.'

It was a curious explanation, but she did not delve deeper while another matter was surging forward in her mind with a great deal more urgency, and she waited until he was seated before she spoke.

'Louis, I know about Marguerite.'

He looked up sharply. 'You know?'

'Julien told me everything.'

'He has remembered?' Louis had a distinctly odd look about him, and the hand that held the glass shook visibly. 'He knows everything?'

'I think you have misunderstood,' she said with a calmness that belied the disturbing awareness that she was on the brink of discovering something important. 'Julien has told me everything he knows, but he still can't recall those hours during which Marguerite died.'

'*Ciel!*' A fine layer of perspiration stood out on his forehead, but Louis had controlled himself with remarkable swiftness. 'For a moment I thought he had remembered everything.'

'Tell me what *you* know about Marguerite,' Emma prompted before Louis could regain his mental balance. 'What was she like?'

'She was beautiful, exciting, and a little wild.'

'And you were in love with her,' she concluded, her suspicions confirmed by that strange glitter she had seen in his eyes when he had spoken of Marguerite.

'*Oui*, I was in love with her,' he admitted with a touch of arrogant bravado before he swallowed down a mouthful of his drink. 'Is it so wrong to love another man's wife?'

'That depends on what happened between you and Marguerite while she was married to Julien.'

A smile played about his tight mouth, but it did not quite reach his dark eyes. 'I think you are trying to trap me.'

'I can only trap you if you have something to hide, Louis, and I'm beginning to think that you have.'

'*Mon Dieu!*' he exclaimed, holding her steady, unwavering glance with his own. 'You are a very shrewd woman, Emma Gilbert, but can I trust you?'

She shrugged with affected casualness, but her eyes did not waver from his while she took a sip of her wine. 'You will have to decide for yourself whether you can trust me, but I have every intention of digging until I find out the truth.'

'The truth!' He went white about the mouth and, putting down his glass, he covered his face with his hands. Someone laughed loudly, and boisterously below his window, and the sound jarred the tense silence in the room as Louis lowered his hands and stared bleakly at the carpet beneath his feet. 'The truth is that Julien and I were both very much in love with Marguerite, but she chose Julien, and I . . .' His mouth twisted with pain, then he swallowed down the remainder of his drink, and got to his feet to pace the floor. 'I stood on the outside adoring her in silence until two and a half years ago. Marguerite was always a little wild and unpredictable, but after Dominic was born she was wilder than ever before, and she was then with this man, then with the other. I was always there, the one she would run to for help, and then, six months before she died, the most incredible thing happened. She told me that she loved me, and after that we saw each other almost every day, meeting secretly at my villa, or in places where we would not be recognised together.'

'Julien wouldn't give her a divorce, I know that,' Emma intervened quietly while her feelings hovered between compassion and distaste.

'No, he would not give her a divorce,' Louis acknowledged grimly, ceasing his senseless pacing and lowering himself into the chair facing Emma. 'It is against his Catholic principles, and he is a man who does not waver from what he believes is right. Marguerite begged him many times to give her her freedom, but always it was the same answer, and on the day she died we had planned to go away together. She went home late that afternoon to pack a few things, and we were to leave that same night on a chartered flight to South Africa. We had both believed that Julien would be staying overnight at the hotel in Tamarin, but he had returned unexpectedly to the villa, and *le bon Dieu* only knows what happened when she arrived there that afternoon.' He pressed shaky fingers against his eyelids before he continued speaking. 'I knew that something was wrong when Marguerite did not arrive at the airport at the time we had arranged, and I drove out to the villa, arriving in time to see the ambulance taking her away. It was Li who told me she was dead, and he asked if I wanted to see Julien, but I refused. I could not face Julien feeling as I did, and I think Li has never forgiven me for it. I am wary of him also. I think he knows too much.'

Several pieces of the puzzle had fallen into place, but the picture was not quite complete. There were still those two blank hours to fill in, and only then would the truth be known in full.

Louis poured himself another drink and, when he turned to face her, he looked exceptionally anxious. 'Are you going to tell Julien what I have just told you?'

'No,' she shook her head, wondering what Julien would think if he should find out that she had delved so deeply into his personal affairs. '*You* should have told him, Louis. You are his friend, and you could have saved him two years of painful soul-searching if you had gone to him and told him about your own involvement.'

Louis' eyebrows rose a fraction. 'You think the shock of hearing about Marguerite and myself may have restored his memory?'

'It may have,' she acknowledged. 'Knowing the truth may have triggered off something in his memory.'

'I could not do it, Emma,' Louis scowled. 'I did not want to hurt him. He is my friend, and I could not do that to him.'

'It's a pity you didn't think of that before you cheated on him by having an affair with his wife,' she reminded him sharply, and he winced visibly.

'You strike very hard where it hurts most, *chérie*,' he smiled ruefully. 'Julien is my friend, but I also loved his wife, and I had to choose.'

'And you chose Marguerite, knowing how heartless she had been in not acknowledging the existence of her own child?' she asked incredulously, deliberately stressing one of Marguerite's most despicable faults.

'*Oui*,' Louis nodded gravely. 'She could be heartless and wild and unpredictable, but I loved her, and nothing else mattered.'

A profound silence followed his disclosure, and Emma was forced to realise that this self-confessed philanderer had truly loved the woman Julien had been married to. That was how she loved Julien, was it not? She loved him, and nothing else mattered beyond that.

'I understand,' she murmured at length, twirling her glass between fingers that trembled slightly.

'*Oui*, I think you do,' Louis said, studying her thoughtfully. 'For you it is Julien, is it not?'

There was no sense in denying it, and she smiled wanly. 'I'm afraid so.'

A strangely sad smile curved his mouth. 'You and I, in some way, are two of a kind, and doomed to love unwisely.'

Doomed to love unwisely. Those words echoed hollowly through her mind, forecasting an empty future, and the thought of it was like a coldness clamping itself about her heart.

'Do you have a photograph of Marguerite?' she changed the subject and, from the drawer of the writing desk, Louis produced a colour photograph of a woman so angelically beautiful that one could not imagine her capable of the things she had done.

Marguerite Perreau's bone structure was perfect, and her tawny eyes were clear and heavily lashed, but her mouth was full and sensual with a faintly petulant curve to the lower lip. Dominic had his mother's eyes and her mouth, but other than that he looked like his father, and Emma wondered how Julien felt each time he looked into his son's eyes. Did he see Marguerite, and was this partly the reason why he behaved so distantly towards Dominic?

'You are quite right, she was beautiful,' Emma said at length as she placed the photograph in Louis' hands, and deep down inside of her there was a pain which could not be assuaged.

What chance did she have with a man like Julien Perreau when he had known and loved a woman as beautiful as Marguerite? Only Daniella Bertrand's sultry beauty might suffice.

Louis ordered a light meal for both of them and, when it was served, they dined in comparative silence. Emma felt peculiarly drained, and Louis looked as if he had suddenly lost his usual vitality. Neither of them was particularly hungry, and Louis took her back to the villa immediately after they had had their coffee.

'Don't get out,' Emma said hastily, placing her hand on Louis' arm when he had parked his car in the villa's driveway. 'Thanks for the dinner, and for being so honest with me.'

Louis did not reply, but he placed his hand over hers, and squeezed it briefly before she got out and closed the door.

Emma watched him drive away, and only then did she turn to mount the steps. Some instinct made her look up when she put her foot on the first step, and her heart missed several suffocating beats when she saw Julien observing her from the patio above her. He looked aggressive with his feet planted firmly apart and his arms crossed over his wide chest, and she sensed silent condemnation as well as anger in his stance. His stillness frightened her considerably, but she pulled herself together and ascended the steps until she stood facing him on the dimly lit patio.

'You have enjoyed your evening with Louis?' he questioned her coldly, his eyes burning into hers as he uncrossed his arms and thrust his clenched hands into the pockets of his beige linen pants.

'Yes, I did,' she said in defiance, although not the complete truth when she detected something distasteful in his query. 'But I didn't enjoy it in the way you may imagine.'

His jaw hardened. 'If you are so clever to read my mind, then how do I imagine you spent the past hours?'

'In his bed,' she said bluntly.

'And am I to believe that you did not?'

She paled and stepped away from him as if he had struck her. 'If you think I'm that sort of woman, then we have nothing more to say to each other, *monsieur*.'

'Emma!' His fingers snaked like a fiery leash about her wrist when she turned to leave. 'I do not have the right to interfere in your free time, but I am concerned for you.'

'You have a strange way of showing your concern when you yourself have treated me abominably. Louis has not so much as laid a finger on me, while you——' She halted abruptly in her reckless tirade to jerk her wrist free of his clasp, and to turn from his intensely probing glance before he saw the glimmer of tears in her eyes. 'Oh, God, why am I standing here saying these things and laying myself wide open for ridicule and more humiliation?' she spoke her thoughts aloud.

His hands gripped her shoulders, and he turned her roughly to face him. 'You think I wish to ridicule and humiliate you?'

'What else am I supposed to think when you—when you make love to me one minute and—and ignore me the next?' She blinked back her tears and raised her angry eyes to his. 'I don't just feel humiliated, I feel used—cheap!'

'*Non*, Emma, that is not so, I——' He released her abruptly, his face grim as he turned from her to lean with his hands against the low wall, and quite suddenly this autocratic man looked so dejected that her anger melted away. '*Mon Dieu!*' he muttered fiercely. 'I am a *man*, and I am *human*, but I have not the right to *you*, or any other woman while I live with the shadow of a death I cannot account for.'

What was he saying? Was he trying to make her see that he cared, but that he considered he did not have the right to feel that way?

'Julien, I——'

The words stilled in her throat when he turned to face her, and his tortured expression told her more in that moment than any words could have done.

'I thought you would understand, and would know how I feel,' he accused in a quiet way which hurt more than if he had spoken harshly, and she winced inwardly despite the joyous pounding of her heart.

'Oh, Julien, I do . . . now.'

Their eyes met for endless, magical moments, then that shuttered, aloof mask shifted over his lean face. 'I am going to have a cognac. Will you join me?'

She should have declined, but the desire to be with him was much stronger. 'If you have a little wine to offer me, yes.'

'Come,' he said abruptly, and she followed him into his study which was once again lit only by the reading lamp. As he crossed the room towards the cabinet in the corner he gestured to an envelope lying on his desk blotter. 'There is a letter for you from South Africa.'

She sensed his suspicion, and found herself up against a wall of cynicism and lack of trust which Marguerite had erected in him. It was almost incredible to believe that a woman of such angelic beauty could create such havoc with a man's life, but Marguerite had succeeded in wrecking the lives of *two* men, and it was perhaps providence that she had been prevented from doing more damage than she had done already.

CHAPTER NINE

EMMA recognised Lucy's handwriting on the envelope, and a mischievous smile sparkled in her eyes, but it was gone again the next instant. She might have considered being tantalisingly evasive about the identity of the writer if the circumstances had been different, and if it had been anyone other than Julien Perreau who had regarded the letter with such suspicion, but this situation called for complete honesty.

'It's a letter from my sister,' Emma explained, turning the envelope idly in her hands while she observed Julien through lowered lashes, and she could sense his fierce battle against disbelief.

'Your sister is married?'

'Yes, Lucy is married.' A smile curved her mouth when she thought of the many times Lucy had contrived to inveigle her into a similar status. 'She's four years my senior, and she has two little girls.'

'Your parents?' Julien questioned, walking towards her with a glass in each hand, and she noticed at once that his manner was more relaxed.

'They died some years ago,' she replied soberly, accepting a glass of wine from him and murmuring her thanks.

'You are very close, you and your sister?'

'Very close,' she smiled, lowering herself into the chair he had indicated, but Julien seated himself on the corner of the desk, and she sensed a certain restlessness in him again.

'You may read your letter, if you wish.'

'Thank you,' she murmured and, placing her glass of

wine on the table beside her, she slipped her thumb beneath the flap of the envelope, and ripped it open.

It was not a long letter, merely two pages and, typical of Lucy, it was brief and to the point.

Dear Emma, Lucy had written. *We have received only one letter from you since your departure. What is happening out there at the villa in Mauritius, and why haven't we heard from you again?*

If only Lucy knew, Emma thought wryly, but she forced herself to concentrate on the rest of the letter. There was news of the children, and Richard's promotion to director of the company he worked for, but on the second page the letter ended abruptly with something close to a threat.

If I don't hear from you within the next three weeks, I have a good mind to send Richard out there to investigate, Lucy had written, and Emma nibbled nervously at her lower lip.

That was all she needed now, she thought agitatedly, and she could imagine the embarrassing fiasco if Richard should storm into the villa demanding to know what had happened to his wife's sister.

'Something is wrong?'

Emma folded the letter carefully, slipping it into the envelope, and taking a careful sip of wine before she answered. 'I'm afraid that the last time I wrote to my sister was shortly after my arrival on the island, and she says that if she doesn't hear from me within the next few weeks she is thinking of sending my brother-in-law out here to investigate.'

A silence settled between them, and Emma drank her wine a little more hurriedly to calm those nerves which were beginning to quiver at the pit of her stomach.

'I can understand their concern,' Julien said at length, draining his glass and staring down into it as if he were surprised to find it empty. 'You are in a strange country, and living with people they do not know. It is natural that your family will be concerned.'

'I'll write to her tonight to set her mind at rest.'

'I suggest that you do,' said Julien sternly, and their eyes met for a brief, electrifying second. 'More wine?'

'No, thank you,' she shook her head and, putting down her glass, she got to her feet. The study was suddenly too small to accommodate both of them simultaneously, and a current of awareness flowed between them which was sparking off feelings she knew had to be subdued. The longing to fling herself into his arms was intense, but it was a longing she had to suppress, and she clung instead to the comforting thought that he had come close to telling her that he cared. Julien stirred suddenly, and she whispered hastily, 'I must go.'

'*Oui*, you must go,' he agreed, shattering the strange spell which had gripped them, and Emma murmured a husky 'goodnight' before going up to her suite.

She wrote a letter to Lucy before going to bed, taking care to give the impression that she was very happy in her new job. She *was* happy, that much was true, but there was also the pain of loving, and the latter was something she dared not mention to Lucy. Emma centred her news on Dominic, and the beauty of the island, but she took great care not to mention Julien Perreau. Later, perhaps, she would write and tell Lucy more about him, but not now, and not while it was possible she could have imagined something which had not been there.

It was not Lucy, but Julien she was thinking of when she lay in bed that evening. Their conversation on the patio whirled through her mind, and she went over it repeatedly in her search for confirmation of what she had imagined, but in the end she had to admit to herself that Julien Perreau had in no way committed himself.

He had spoken of hoping that she understood and would know how he felt, but he could have been referring to anything, and not necessarily what she had imagined.

'Oh, Julien, Julien,' she breathed his name despairingly, and he was still in her thoughts when she at last went to sleep.

Emma was determined to see Reggie again, and during the next few days she made a practise of going for long, slow walks through the garden after lunch. She lingered for more than an hour sometimes close to the tree where she had encountered him before, but Reggie did not put in an appearance. She repeated this ritual for more than a week, and she was beginning to lose hope when a movement in the foliage above her caught her eye one afternoon.

'*Mademoiselle!*' Reggie's voice called to her from his perch high up in the tree. 'You are alone?'

'Quite alone, I assure you,' she replied, pausing beneath the tree and craning her neck to see him.

His dark face peered down at her through the branches. 'You did not tell Monsieur Perreau that I come here?'

'I didn't tell him anything,' she assured the child. 'You were here again almost two weeks ago, weren't you? When I was in the garden with Dominic?'

'*Oui,*' Reggie replied, making no attempt to climb down.

'Why did you run away?'

'I speak to you alone.'

'Well, if you're going to speak to me, then I suggest you come down here,' she invited when she felt her neck muscles begin to ache, and Reggie cast a swift, searching glance across the garden before he began his descent.

Emma sat down on a fallen log and, when Reggie dropped to the ground, she gestured that he should sit down beside her. He was a slender boy, all arms and legs, and big dark eyes from which that look of fear never departed entirely. She felt sorry for him, and most especially so when she thought of his father. Sammy Moodley, in his quest for revenge, had succeeded in frightening Reggie considerably, and Emma could almost hate him for doing something so despicable to a child.

'My rabbit she have eight babies,' Reggie informed her gravely when he sat down beside her and stretched his thin legs out in front of him.

'That's nice,' she smiled, but she spoke automatically while her mind was centred on the plan of action she had prepared. 'What colour are they?'

'Some white, and some white with black spots,' he said, picking up a stick and drawing squiggles in the loose soil beneath their feet.

Emma studied him closely, and decided there was no sense in delaying what had to be done. 'I climbed this tree the other day, Reggie, and I could see all the way on to the patio of the villa.'

'I must go,' he said, leaping to his feet, and the fear in his eyes served to confirm her suspicions.

'Sit down, Reggie,' she instructed quietly, clutching at his arm with her fingers and urging him to resume his seat beside her. 'Trust me, and don't be afraid.'

He shook his head. 'I not afraid of you.'

'I would like you to trust me as well.'

Uncertainty and fear still lurked in his eyes when he stared at her, but she felt the muscles relax in his thin arm. 'I trust you.'

'Good,' she breathed easier, but she left her hand on his arm, determined not to let him escape until they had thrashed this matter out to the bitter end. 'Now, I want 'ou to listen to me, Reggie, because this is very mportant, and I want you to tell me the truth.'

'I listen,' he said, and Emma held her breath as she shot up a silent little prayer for help.

'You had climbed this tree one day about two years ago, and you happened to see something on the patio,' she chose the direct approach, and the result was startling.

'Non, non!' Reggie cried, his eyes like saucers, and his face paling beneath the darkness of his skin, but, surprisingly, he made no attempt to escape from her.

'You went home to your father, and you told him what you had seen because you were frightened,' she pressed on with the conclusions she had reached since their last meeting, and she could see that she was hitting the mark each time.

'Non, mademoiselle, non!'

'Your father told you not to talk to anyone about what you had seen, and he threatened that he would beat you, or something equally drastic if you didn't obey him.' Emma studied him intently. 'That is so, isn't it?'

'Non!' he protested, but she could sense that he was weakening.

'Reggie, listen to me,' she said quietly, but firmly. 'Monsieur Perreau cannot remember what happened that day, and it is making him very unhappy. If you know the truth, Reggie, then you must tell me what you saw.'

Reggie stared fixedly at the ground, and Emma gave him time to consider, but she had never been so tense, nor so scared in all her life. The information she sought from this child was of indescribable importance and, if she failed now, she might never have another opportunity to question him. His fear of his father's wrath would make him avoid the villa as if the plague had erupted in its grounds, and Julien might have to live for ever with the guilty knowledge that he migh have driven his wife to her death.

'Reggie . . .' She leaned towards him, the very softness of her voice stressing the urgency of the matter 'Tell me the truth, and I promise that your father wil never know about it. Trust me . . . please?'

He turned his head to look at her, and what he saw in her eyes must have convinced him that she was sincere. His taut body relaxed slowly until he sa in a slouched position, and Emma found hersel holding her breath when he nodded slowly i agreement.

'I—I see *monsieur* and *madame* on the patio,' he began haltingly.

'Yes?' Emma prodded softly, her heart thumping in her breast at the thought of what she was about to hear and there was also an undeniable thread of fear coiling its way through her.

'They talk,' Reggie continued. 'I cannot hear, but I see they talk. *Madame* she is very angry, and she beat *monsieur* . . . like this.' He clenched his fists and demonstrated where words failed him. '*Monsieur* take her hands to stop her, but she pull her hands free, and then she fall. *Monsieur* rush to catch her, but his foo slip on top step, and he fall to the side to beat his head on the wall.'

'And Madame Perreau?' Emma prompted, her hear beating in her throat with a force that almost choked her.

'She fall down steps like so.' Reggie gestured with his hands to give the impression of someone tumbling head over heels. 'And she lie very still, just like Monsieu Perreau,' he concluded his explanation.

'Oh, my God!' Emma breathed in something between relief and horror, and there was excitement there as well. At last she had something with which to confront Julien in the hope of jogging his memory.

'I go now?'

'Yes, Reggie,' Emma smiled shakily. 'You may go.'

'You tell my father, and he beat me,' he warned, the fear returning to his eyes.

'I shan't tell your father.' She raised her hand in a solemn gesture which she knew he would understand. 'On my word of honour.'

A smile broke through the severity of his expression. *'Sallam, mademoiselle.'*

'Sallam,' she responded, but Reggie had already darted over the wall, and then he was gone.

The final, most devastating piece of the puzzle had at last fallen into place, or so Emma thought. Except for his feelings of guilt, Julien could be free; free to live, and free to love. She sobered at the thought. Would he ever love again, or would he choose with the mind this time, instead of the heart?

'Emma?' Dominic questioned her that evening when she put him to bed. 'Something is wrong?'

'No, darling,' she laughed, scooping him rather impulsively into her arms and kissing him on his cheek. 'Everything is so very right,' she added optimistically.

'You are happy?' he asked, locking his arms about her neck.

'Yes, I'm happy,' she confessed, but she silently admitted to herself at last that she was also afraid.

She could not ignore the fact that *she* was the one who would have to enlighten Julien, and not knowing how he would react to the truth frightened her. Would he be overjoyed, or would it shatter him? He might even be annoyed with her for delving so deeply into what he considered his personal life. She was, after all, employed by him as Dominic's governess, and a few kisses and a little lovemaking did not alter her position in his household.

Emma had never felt less like eating when she went down to dinner that evening. Her mind was bursting with the information Reggie had passed on to her, and sheer nerves clutched at her stomach in a way which left little room for the grilled tuna which had been marinated in coconut oil. Celestine tried to tempt Emma with her favourite salad, but Emma declined, knowing that she could barely manage what she already had on her plate. Her unobtrusive glance darted repeatedly in Julien's direction where he sat at the head of the table. His features wore that familiar cold, expressionless mask, but it was what lay hidden behind that mask that interested Emma. What was he thinking? And what would he do when she confronted him with the truth?

She excused herself from the table as soon as she could, and looked in on Dominic before going to her suite. Dominic was asleep with one hand curled in under his cheek and, in a rush of tenderness, she bent over him to kiss him lightly on the forehead. He did not stir, and she stood there staring down at him with a smile on her lips. She had grown more than simply fond of him during the past three months, and the mere thought of having to go away from him sent a stab of pain through her insides and a constricting lump to her throat.

Sighing heavily, she switched off Dominic's bedside light and walked quietly out of his room to go to her suite where she had decided to wait until the hour Julien usually retired to his study.

Emma had often wondered what Julien did there in his study every night when he was not out somewhere on business, or having dinner with Daniella Bertrand. His business interests were so varied that she could imagine there would be a tremendous amount of paper work involved, and she had not been on the island for almost three months without discovering that Julien had offices in Port Louis as well as Curepipe, and both were complete with secretaries and accountants. She also knew that Julien commuted almost daily between the sugar plantation, the Hotel de Soleil at Tamarin, and his main office in Curepipe from where he kept a strict control on every aspect of his business affairs.

The study light was switched on some minutes later. From her window she could see a soft light spreading out across that particular section of the patio, and her heart began to bounce uncomfortably in her throat. This was the moment she had been waiting for, and now she was suddenly so scared that her courage almost failed her. She had harboured such positive feelings about her actions, but now she was being besieged by doubts. Breaking open that sealed door in Julien's mind was something which would eventually involve several people. There was Louis, Reggie, and Sammy Moodley. Emma did not care much what happened to Sammy, but she was concerned for Louis, and she was concerned also for Reggie. She knew that she had to get her priorities in order, and her logical mind told her it was important that Julien should know the truth, but her heart was concerned only with the repercussions which might follow. Her mind finally won the silent battle, and she went downstairs to do what she knew had to be done.

'*Entrez,*' Julien answered her tentative knock a few minutes later, and her hand was shaking when she opened the door.

'Are you very busy?' she asked, her glance sliding over the multitude of papers in front of him.

'*Non,*' he said abruptly, putting down his pen and

pushing his chair a little away from the desk. 'You have something you wish to discuss with me?'

'Yes, I do.'

'Then do not stand there hovering,' he ordered harshly. 'Come in and close the door.'

He was, in that moment, not the man she loved, but her austere and autocratic employer, and that invisible barrier between them was almost tangible in the warm night air that filtered in through the open patio doors. It made her feel ill at ease, but most of all it hurt.

'*Monsieur* ...' she began, closing the door and stepping farther into the room.

'Julien,' he corrected her halting approach to what she had to tell him, and a derisive smile curved his mouth. 'You have called me Julien for some time, and I see no reason to alter that.'

Her cheeks flamed, and she avoided the stabbing mockery in his eyes when they travelled the length of her and forced her to recall certain moments of intimacy between them which she would much rather have forgotten.

'Julien, I——' She swallowed convulsively and gathered her scattered wits about her. There was no sense in rushing headlong into an explanation, and it might be safer to exercise a certain degree of caution. 'I think I have a pretty good idea of what happened that day on the patio when Marguerite died.'

She had chosen her words carefully, but the ensuing silence was so intense that when the clock on the trophy cabinet struck the half hour it had the effect of a cannon being fired at close quarters.

'I can most certainly do without your speculations, Emma,' he warned in an ominously quiet voice as he pushed back his chair and got to his feet.

'This is more than speculation,' she assured him while

he walked towards the patio doors and lit a cheroot. 'You were seen that day.'

His formidable back stiffened. 'By whom?'

'Sammy Moodley's son,' she informed him, holding her breath almost as she spoke.

'Reggie?' He swung round sharply, his brows meeting in a frown above his dark, incredulous eyes. 'I do not believe this. How could he have witnessed the incident, and, if this is so, then why did he not come to me two years ago with this information when it was made known that I could not recall what happened?'

'To answer your first question,' she explained, swallowing nervously. 'Reggie was perched in a tree at the bottom end of the garden, and I climbed it myself to discover that one had an excellent view of the patio. To answer your second question is not quite so simple. Reggie must have been frightened by what he had seen that day, and he naturally rushed home to tell his father. He could only have been about ten years old at the time, so his fear was understandable, but he has lived since with an even greater fear. Sammy had forbidden Reggie to speak of what he had seen, and Reggie is terrified that his father may find out he has spoken to me.'

Julien frowned down at the cheroot dangling between his fingers as if he had no clear recollection of how it had got there, then he raised his head, and his dark eyes stabbed at her with a hint of wariness in their depths.

'What did Reggie see that day?'

Emma's palms felt cold and damp despite the humid warmth of the night. 'Before I tell you anything, Julien, I want you to give me your word that, whatever you decide to do, you will not involve Reggie.'

'I give you my word that I shall not involve Reggie,' he agreed solemnly, then impatience harshened his voice.

'*Mon Dieu*, Emma, tell me what he saw and let us not beat about the bush a moment longer!'

'He saw you on the patio with Marguerite.'

'That much I have gathered,' he intervened with harsh sarcasm, drawing hard on his cheroot, and crushing the remainder into the marble ashtray on the circular table close to him.

'Marguerite was apparently very angry, and she was beating at you with her fists,' Emma related what Reggie had told her. 'You grabbed her wrists to stop her, but she broke free and must have lost her balance in the process. You tried to prevent her from falling, but your foot slipped on the top step, and you fell to the side, knocking your head against the wall.' Her heart was in her eyes, but he was blind to it at that moment when she stressed the importance of what she had told him. 'If at any time you may have harboured certain doubts, then you may now rest assured that you didn't *push* her, Julien. It was an *accident*.'

'*Mon Dieu!*' he groaned, and his face was ashen as he slumped into the nearest chair.

'Julien?' She went to his side at once, and his eyes had a glazed look that frightened her when she kneeled down beside his chair and placed an anxious hand on his arm. 'Julien, are you all right?'

'*Oui,*' he assured her in a hoarse voice, but she doubted his statement when she saw the whiteness linger beneath his tanned complexion.

'Perhaps I should call the doctor.'

'*Non,*' he stopped her at once. 'There is no need for a doctor.'

She stared at him, heart thumping and frightened almost out of her wits by his paleness, then she left his side to dash across the room and, with a hand that shook, she poured a double tot of cognac into a glass.

'Here, drink this,' she whispered anxiously, recalling

that night he had given her cognac to calm her. She placed the glass in his hand and watched him closely when he swallowed down the first mouthful of the amber-coloured liquid.

'*Merci,*' he murmured at length, the glazed look leaving his eyes, but he still had that frightened hint of paleness about the mouth.

'Are you sure you don't want me to call the doctor?' she questioned him tentatively once more, but he shook his head.

'I am sure. I do not need the doctor.'

Emma lowered herself into the chair facing him, but she continued to watch him closely. It was shock, she realised that, and she cursed herself silently for not consulting with the doctor before she bombarded Julien with the facts. She had been an idiot, but it was too late now to do anything about it. She wanted to hold him, to comfort him, but she dared not even do that, and she sat there swamped with helpless misery. She could see his torment and she could feel it, but she could not help him, and neither could she understand it.

'Has the information I have given you helped in any way?' she questioned him eventually.

'I can remember nothing,' he confirmed what she had begun to suspect. 'I want to believe what you have told me, but I can remember nothing.'

'Give your mind the opportunity to adjust to this knowledge, and it will all come back to you in time,' she tried to reassure him, but she did not sound very convincing even to herself.

'If it is true that I struggled with Marguerite on the steps that day, then why can I not remember, and why does nothing you say sound familiar to me?'

'I wish I had the answer to that, but I don't,' she admitted reluctantly, lowering her eyes to her clenched hands. 'I can only hope that, when the shock of what I have told you has worn off, you will find yourself recalling the details for yourself.'

'You are optimistic, *chérie*,' he mocked her, in complete control of himself again. 'Did it not occur to you that Reggie may have lied to you?'

She had believed Reggie so implicitly that this thought had never crossed her mind, and she refused to dwell on the possibility that the boy had lied to her. 'He was telling the truth.'

'You are a very determined young woman, and I would imagine that you exerted a little pressure to get the information you required from Reggie.' He smiled twistedly into her startled eyes. 'Am I right?'

'In a way, yes, but——'

'If he fears his father as much as you say, then it is possible that he may have lied to you in order to escape the punishment his father had threatened him with.'

'*No!*' she stated emphatically, her mind rejecting his suggestion with some distaste. 'He told me the truth! I know it!'

Julien sat forward in his chair and studied her intently with his elbows resting on his knees. His eyes defied her to avoid his piercing glance, and she felt like a moth being hypnotised by the flame of a candle.

'Is it so important to you to prove my innocence beyond doubt?' he asked at length without taking his eyes from hers, and her heart skipped an uncomfortable beat somewhere in her throat.

'Isn't your own peace of mind important to you?' she counter-questioned evasively. 'Isn't it enough that you feel guilty about not giving Marguerite the divorce she had wanted?'

'You have not answered my question, Emma.'

She felt trapped. The truth was the only answer she could give him, and she could not decide whether she dared risk baring her soul to this man. He was demanding far too much of her, and in return she would receive nothing from him to feed the hungry longing in her heart.

'Yes, it is important to me to prove your innocence and lighten your burden,' she said eventually, getting up agitatedly, but Julien's hand shot out to latch on to her wrist before she could move away from him, and she was pulled down on to her knees at his feet.

'Why?' he demanded softly, the very quietness of his voice a command she could not ignore. 'Why is it important to you?'

Emma could not look at him and, fixing her gaze on the silver crucifix about his neck, she said in a husky whisper, 'It's important because I can't bear to see you live under this shadow of Marguerite's death, and because I can't stand to see you torment yourself with guilt.'

He released her wrist to push his hands through the silken mass of her hair, and a gentle tug was enough to force her to meet the burning intensity of his gaze. 'I have managed to live with my guilt for two years.'

'You haven't *lived*, Julien,' she argued fiercely. 'You have merely *existed* by burying yourself in your work, and by shutting yourself away from those closest to you. You have denied yourself everything. You have even denied yourself the love of your mother and your son, and I think you will never stop denying yourself the right to live while you allow that cloak of guilt to smother all your natural feelings.'

He stared at her with an unfathomable expression in his eyes, then he pulled her up between his knees, and she went into his arms with an eagerness she knew she would despise herself for later. His mouth trailed fiery kisses across her throat and, when his lips found hers, she melted against him with no thought of resistance in her mind. Her hands shifted up from his waist to cling to his shoulders, and for endless seconds nothing existed beyond the wonder and the magic of his kisses, but she could not ignore the hint of desperation in the way his hands moved against her back.

Like everything else this moment had to end, and he held her away from him to look down at her raised face with pain in his eyes. 'Will you leave me now, *s'il vous plaît?*'

A protest rose to her lips, but she bit it back and rose to her feet. 'Yes, of course.'

'And, Emma . . .' he stopped her before she reached the door. 'I appreciate what you tried to do.'

Emma felt choked. She had achieved nothing except to add to his innumerable doubts, and the frustration of finding herself up against that immovable wall brought the sting of tears to her eyes.

'I didn't do very much, I'm afraid,' she murmured miserably and, turning from him before he could see the tears brimming in her eyes, she walked out of his study and stumbled rather blindly up the stairs.

On the top landing she almost collided with Celestine Perreau, and the unexpectedness of the meeting left Emma no time to hide the tears which were now spilling on to her cheeks.

'What is the matter, *chérie?*'

'Oh, *madame*,' Emma croaked, unable to keep her failure to herself. 'I discovered something which I thought would help Julien, but I think I have simply succeeded in making matters worse.'

'Come,' Madame Perreau commanded gently. 'We will go to your suite, and you will tell me all about it.'

Emma did not argue. It would be a relief to talk to someone, and at that moment Celestine Perreau was the most appropriate person she could think of.

In the privacy of her lounge she told Julien's mother about her meetings with Reggie Moodley, and what she had learned from him. She told her also of Julien's reaction to this information, and she ended with a despairing, 'I have failed miserably, *madame*.'

'How can you say that you have failed?' Celestine rebuked her gently. 'Only time will tell, and who knows what tomorrow may bring.'

Emma looked up sharply. 'Do *you* believe what Reggie told me?'

'I do not know what to believe, but I have faith in you, Emma,' she smiled. 'If anyone can help my son, then I know it is you.'

'*Madame* . . .'

'You have given your heart to my son, have you not?'

Emma felt that tell-tale warmth surging into her cheeks, and she lowered her eyes hastily. '*Madame*, I . . . I don't know what to say.'

'There is no need for you to say anything, *chérie*,' she said with a smile in her voice as her fingers gently squeezed Emma's arm. 'For a long time now I have seen the way you look at him, but Julien, I think, is too blind to see when a woman has her heart in her eyes.'

'*Madame*, I——'

She gestured Emma to silence and got to her feet. 'Make my son alive again, Emma, and you will have my blessing.'

Long after Madame Celestine had gone Emma still sat there with those words ringing in her ears. 'Make my son alive again, and you will have my blessing.'

Make my son alive again.

Oh, God! If only she could!

CHAPTER TEN

THERE was something odd about Julien, and it puzzled Emma during the days that followed. His eyes glittered strangely, as if he had a fever, but other than that he did not look ill. His features looked grim at times, and he spoke very little, but he seemed to unbend more towards Dominic. Emma was pleased about the latter even though her spirits were low, and it touched her heart to see Dominic slowly discard his wariness of his father during those brief moments they spent together in the evenings at bedtime.

Daniella Bertrand came to dinner one evening, and once again Madame Celestine's displeasure was evident in the tightening of her mouth. Emma, too, had a premonition of something unpleasant about to happen, and her misery deepened when she sensed a shared excitement between Julien and Daniella at the dinner table. Their conversation lapsed naturally into French when the coffee had been served, but Emma had picked up sufficient from Dominic to understand what they were saying, and she followed the discussion in silence.

They had mentioned the fact that the Royal College at Curepipe would soon be closing for the April holidays, and Daniella's manicured hand found its usual resting place on Julien's arm.

'Ah, *mon cher*, there is so much I am looking forward to. This will be our first flight together, and——' She paused abruptly when he gestured reprovingly with his hand, but it was too late, and there was an odd tension around the table when Daniella asked with a measure of surprise, 'You have not told your mother?'

'*Non*,' Julien answered her abruptly, and Daniella's expression was at once apologetic.

'Excuse *moi, mon cher*, I have spoken out of turn.'

Emma felt a dreaded coldness settle about her heart as Celestine Perreau put down her cup and asked directly, 'What have you not told me, Julien?'

Julien and Daniella exchanged brief, telling glances, then Julien met his mother's direct gaze. 'I am taking the afternoon flight to South Africa tomorrow, and I cannot say when I shall return.'

'Daniella is going with you?'

'We are going together, *oui*,' he confirmed.

'You are going for business reasons?' Celestine probed.

'*Non, Maman*,' Julien smiled faintly. 'I cannot explain now my reasons for this unexpected trip to South Africa, but when I have returned it shall all be explained, and then you will understand.'

The tension in the atmosphere did not diminish, and the ensuing silence was finally broken when Daniella addressed Julien in English with a rebuke in her voice. 'We are speaking French, *mon cher*, and that is not nice when there is someone with us who cannot follow what we are saying.'

'There is no need for you to translate your conversation,' Emma assured her stiffly. 'Dominic has been an excellent teacher, and I hope the same can be said for myself where his English is concerned.' She saw Julien's eyebrows rise a fraction in surprise, but she excused herself and left the dining-room before he could voice the mockery she had seen in his eyes.

When she reached the sanctuary of her suite there was a tightness in her chest which was born of a fear she could not explain, and she walked across the darkened lounge to stand listlessly in front of the open window. She drew the warm, scented air into her lungs and told herself not to be ridiculous. She had imagined something which was not there, she tried to tell herself, but she was not entirely convinced.

Emma had no idea how long she had stood there before she became aware of the murmur of voices below her window, and she leaned forward carefully to see Julien and Daniella's shadows stretched out across the patio in the light which shone out from the study.

'*Mon amour,*' Daniella was saying in her sultry voice which she reserved for Julien. 'I apologise again for speaking out of turn, but we have also been a little naughty in not telling them the truth.'

'They will know when the formalities have been dealt with, and not before,' Julien replied firmly.

'Sometimes I am a devil, but you are a devil most of the time,' Daniella accused.

Julien's mocking laughter drifted up towards Emma, and the sound of it made her feel as if she had become frozen in every limb. She saw their shadows merge to become one on the patio, and she stepped back from the window with a stifled cry of anguish on her lips.

'Oh, God, no . . . *no!*' she groaned softly, and a wave of pain washed over her with a near unbearable force.

She stumbled from the lounge into her bedroom on legs that moved in an uncoordinated fashion, and she sat down heavily on her bed without switching on the light. She was cold despite the warmth of the night, and she shivered uncontrollably. She wished that she could cry, but no tears came and, unable to prevent the shivers, she wrapped her arms about herself and sat there nursing her deep-seated misery. Julien was taking a flight to South Africa with Daniella. At this precise moment they were downstairs in his study, locked in an embrace, and probably making plans which involved only the two of them. *No!* Emma did not want to think about it, but her mind was like a dog with a bone which it would not release.

Julien and Daniella were planning their marriage. What else could he have meant when he spoke of the formalities which had to be dealt with? There was a dark, throbbing pain in Emma's breast, and she wished at that moment that she could die. But dying was not so easy. She would have to go on living, and that was something she dreaded. When she thought of Julien bringing Daniella back to the villa as his wife it was like being tormented in hell, and she felt the agonising fire of it searing through her at that very moment.

Emma Gilbert, you're crazy! Lucy's voice leapt into her tortured mind, and she wished now that she had listened to her sister. She should have stuck to her safe and secure existence. None of this would have happened if she had not latched on to the crazy idea that she wanted more out of life than simply teaching. She would never have met Julien, and she would never have known the joy and pain of loving. She would have gone on from day to day as she had done before, and one day she may have met someone, but in her heart she knew that in Julien she had found that once in a lifetime love which could never be replaced.

'Oh, God!' she moaned into the darkness. 'Why did it have to happen to me!'

Her body felt cold and damp when she undressed herself and crawled into bed. She wanted desperately to lose herself in the oblivion of sleep, but instead she lay awake until dawn, and when the first ray of sunshine spilled through her window she was conscious of a numbness where her heart ought to be. She felt empty and drained of feeling, and she thanked God for it.

Emma did not see Julien before his departure that day, and in a way she was thankful for it. She could not face him; not while everything inside her felt so numb and yet so incredibly raw. She needed the weekend to adapt herself, and to come to terms with the inevitable.

Celestine was tight-lipped and silent at the dinner table that Thursday evening, and she remained that way as the weekend dragged on endlessly. Emma could imagine what she was thinking. Were her own thoughts not the same? *Dammit*, she had been determined not to dwell on the subject. It had been sufficient torture seeing Julien and Daniella's shadows merging on the patio, and she dared not let her mind wander farther than that.

Dominic talked of nothing else but his *Papa*'s flight to Durban and, while Dominic looked forward to his father's return, Emma found herself dreading it with every fibre of her being.

They had no idea when he would return, but she was strolling in the garden with Dominic on the Monday afternoon when the Bentley entered the driveway, and Dominic let out a shriek of excitement beside Emma.

'*Papa* is back!' he cried, dashing across the lawn towards the car when it stopped in front of the villa. '*Papa!*'

Julien got out of the Bentley, his immaculate grey suit accentuating his leanness, and he caught Dominic in his arms to lift him high in the air. Dominic's happy laughter tugged at Emma's heart, but her legs felt as if they had been filled with lead when she walked towards them. Daniella was not with Julien, and Emma imagined that he had decided to enlighten Celestine of his marriage before bringing his new wife to the villa.

Oh, God! She was letting her imagination run away with her again, but the numbness left her for the first time in days, and a fresh stab of pain shot through her.

'*Bonjour*, Emma,' Julien greeted her when he had lowered Dominic to the paved driveway, and Emma succeeded in meeting his dark glance without flinching.

'*Bonjour, monsieur,*' she responded, outwardly cool and calm, and one questioning eyebrow rose sharply at her formal address, but the sound of approaching footsteps made him turn to face the woman descending the steps.

'Julien!' Celestine welcomed him in true French style with a kiss on both cheeks.

Emma stared in amazement at Madame Celestine. The tight-lipped expression was gone, and Emma was made to realise that this woman truly cared about her son and, regardless of what he might have chosen to do with his life, she was happy he had arrived home safely.

'Ah, *Maman*,' Julien smiled mockingly. 'It pleases me to know that Dominic is not the only one who is happy to see me.'

'What nonsense is this?' Celestine exclaimed. 'We are all very happy to see you are home safely, are we not, Emma?'

'Yes, of course, *madame*,' Emma muttered tritely, taking Dominic by the hand. 'Come, it is time for your bath.'

Dominic did not argue, but he hung back to glance at his father. 'I missed you, *Papa*.'

'I missed you too, *mon enfant*,' Julien smiled down at him, and his hand went out to ruffle Dominic's hair. 'I will come up later to wish you goodnight.'

Emma felt Julien's eyes following them into the house, and only when they reached Dominic's bedroom did she breathe a little easier, but she could not rid herself of Julien's image. It swam tantalisingly before her eyes, and it made her wonder. In all the time she had been living there at the villa she had seldom seen him smile, yet after this mysterious trip to South Africa he was smiling as if something had occurred there to rid him partly of the shadow he had been living with for so long.

God forgive me, she cried inwardly. *I wanted him to be happy, and I have no right to deny him that happiness with someone else. If Daniella can make him happy, then I will, in time, learn to accept what fate has dealt out for me.*

She felt considerably calmer after that silent prayer, but it did not ease the ache in her heart entirely, and it was with an effort that she concentrated on Dominic to make sure that he bathed himself properly and ate the meal which Nada had brought up to his room for him.

Emma was putting Dominic to bed when the bedroom door opened, and her heart leapt in that old familiar way when Julien entered the room and approached the bed.

'So, you are still awake, Dominic.'

'Papa!' Dominic sat up in bed and pointed excitedly towards the large parcel Julien held in his hands. 'What have you there?'

'It is a present for you.'

'Oh!' Dominic smiled eagerly, his tawny eyes riveted to the gaily wrapped box.

Julien's arm brushed accidentally against Emma's when the gift exchanged hands, and she drew back sharply at the surge of feeling that swept through her at that brief contact. She could not bear to be so close to him and yet so far away, and she had to get out of that room while her trembling legs would still allow it.

'If you will excuse me, I——'

'There is no need for you to leave, Emma,' Julien interrupted her at once while Dominic tore the wrappings off the parcel.

'If you don't mind, *monsieur*, I would like to bath and change before dinner,' she explained, avoiding his probing glance. 'Goodnight, Dominic.'

'Bonne nuit, Emma,' Dominic responded, but his attention was on the electrically operated car which he had removed from the box, and she left his room quickly.

Emma sat through dinner that evening with the feeling that she was perched on a barrel of explosives which could go off at any minute. She expected Julien to make some sort of announcement, but nothing happened, and the conversation was mainly about mundane things such as the weather in Durban over the weekend, and the pleasantness of his flight there and back.

Afraid to be alone with him. Emma excused herself and went up to her suite immediately after dinner. Something, a sixth sense perhaps, warned her that Julien might seek her out, so she went to bed early and switched off her light, but she could not sleep while every nerve in her body was tense and leaping wildly at the slightest sound. She had no idea what she was afraid of, but she knew that she would not be able to bear it if Julien came to her and told her about his marriage, or his intended marriage to Daniella Bertrand. Everyone had their limits, and Emma had most certainly reached hers.

A tap on the door to her suite made her start in bed an hour later and, when she did not respond to it, the knock was repeated sharply. Emma hardly dared to breathe, and panic surged through her when she heard the door being opened. The interleading door stood open, making it easy for him to see that her bedroom was in darkness, and she prayed desperately that he would think she was asleep. If he came any closer he might hear the wild thundering of her heart, and he would know she was faking. *Oh, God, don't let him come any closer!*

'Emma?' his voice called softly, and she bit down hard on her lip to prevent herself from making a sound.

It could only have been a matter of seconds, but it had felt like an eternity before she heard the door close. She maintained a rigid silence for some time before she was certain that he had gone, and only then did she begin to relax.

Julien had already left for his office in Port Louis when Emma went down to breakfast the following morning, and she was relieved that he was not there when Celestine remarked upon the shadows beneath her eyes.

'I have a headache, *madame*,' Emma explained away the visible signs of her restless night, and it was not entirely a lie. Her head had felt heavy since that evening Daniella had dined at the villa, and lack of sleep had not exactly helped to alleviate it.

Dominic kept her busy most of the day, but when evening came her tension increased. She succeeded once again in avoiding Julien, but she knew that she would not always be able to do so, and their eventual confrontation was something she was not looking forward to.

Emma was not in the right mood for sight-seeing on her free afternoon, and she chose to shop around instead for the few personal items she required. Li took her to Curepipe in the Bentley, and dropped her off close to the shopping centre.

'I shall be here at five-thirty, *mademoiselle*,' he warned unnecessarily before he drove away, and Emma smiled to herself as she crossed the street. One of Li's virtues was his absolute punctuality and, although it amused her, it was something she admired.

Curepipe was situated on the central plateau of the island and, because of its altitude, it was always much cooler there than along the coast. Li had taken her once to the *Trou aux Cerfs*, an extinct volcanic crater about three kilometres from Curepipe, and she had found the air up there distinctly chilly, but it had been a clear day and she had been able to see the island of Réunion which lay far to the south-west of Mauritius.

Emma shivered suddenly, but it was not because of the remembered chill in the air when she had stood on the rim of the crater. Could it be a premonition of something unpleasant that lay ahead of her?

'Don't be ridiculous!' she scolded herself and, checking her list, she went in search of the few items she required.

Li welcomed her with a smile and a low bow when she met him again at five-thirty sharp that afternoon, and she slid quickly into the back seat of the car, anxious now to get back to the villa. The hum of the engine was soothing, and she leaned back comfortably, but everything within her leapt to attention when the Bentley shot past the Cap Malheureux turn-off to race on towards Phoenix.

'Li, this isn't the way back to the villa.'

'That is correct, *mademoiselle*.' His slanted eyes smiled at her in the rear view mirror. 'I am not taking you back to the villa.'

Emma felt the coldness of dread sliding into her veins. 'May I know where you are taking me?'

'I am taking you to the *Hôtel du Soleil Levant* at Tamarin where Monsieur Julien awaits you.'

'Oh, no!' she cried in alarm, leaning forward to clutch the seat in front of her. 'Please turn the car around and take me back to the villa. *Please*, Li.'

'I am sorry, *mademoiselle*.' His eyes in the mirror were genuinely apologetic. 'I have my instructions from Monsieur Julien.'

'But I don't——' She broke off abruptly and bit her lip until it ached, then she sagged back in her seat. 'Oh, what's the use!'

Emma had never felt so helpless. She was trapped in the Bentley, it was speeding her towards disaster, and there was nothing she could do about it.

They arrived in Tamarin a half hour later, and he introduction to Julien's *Hotel of The Rising Sun* wa both a pleasure and a pain. The building was a paradis of modern engineering and technology set among palm and green lawns which sloped down to the sandy beac where the crystal clear waters of the Indian Ocean gentl lapped the shore.

'Please, *mademoiselle*,' Li said, opening the door fo her when he had parked the Bentley at the magnificer entrance to the hotel, and she found herself climbin out hesitantly. 'This way, *s'il vous plaît*.'

'What if I refuse?' she asked, making no attempt t follow him towards the swivel door where an elderl couple had emerged moments earlier for a lat afternoon stroll on the beach.

'Mademoiselle Emma,' Li smiled humorously, usin her name for the first time and shaking his head. 'I ma be small, but I am very strong, and I have orders t take you to Monsieur Julien even if I have to use forc to carry out his instructions.'

'It's all right, Li.' She raised her hands in a gestur of abject surrender when he stepped towards he purposefully. 'Only a fool wouldn't know whe they're beaten.'

She accompanied Li into the hotel, but her heart sa somewhere in her throat, and she was blind to th elegance of her surroundings as she preceded Li int the lift and was swept up to the third floor.

Li stood beside her silently, and when the lift doo slid open she was led down a passage and into spacious lounge furnished in soft brown and beige. I she had harboured thoughts of taking flight, then sh was forced to shelve them, for Li stood guard over he until the interleading door opened and Julien steppe into the room.

'Ah, Emma!' he smiled mockingly as Li bowe

imself out and left them alone. 'I am happy to see that
Li succeeded in bringing you here safely.'

In cream linen slacks and tan-coloured shirt his
masculine appeal had never been more potent, but
Emma steeled herself against the magnetism he exuded,
and clutched the strap of her shoulder bag with both
hands as if it were her steadying anchor.

'In certain circles this could be termed as abduction,'
he accused coldly, and Julien's eyebrows rose sharply.

'Li had to use physical measures to bring you here?'

'That wasn't necessary, but in my book it's still
abduction,' she argued stubbornly.

'I have wanted to speak to you privately, and you
have been avoiding me.'

'That's not true,' she lied bravely.

'It is true, and you know it.'

She lowered her lashes guiltily, and at that moment
he knew only the desire to have this confrontation over
and done with as quickly as possible. 'Why have you
had me brought here?'

'We have several matters to discuss, Emma.'

'Such as?'

'Such as you and I, and the future,' he replied
smoothly. 'But first we will have some wine, I think.'

Her legs felt horribly weak beneath her, and she
lowered herself hastily into a chair, but she sat stiffly on
the edge of it until Julien stood in front of her with a
glass of wine in his hand.

'Thank you,' she murmured politely and, in her
attempt to avoid touching his fingers, she almost spilled
some of the crimson liquid into her lap when she
accepted the glass from him.

'Relax, *chérie*,' he ordered tersely, 'And do not look
at me with so much ice in your lovely blue eyes.'

'I feel like a prisoner who has been brought before
the jury.'

'You are not a prisoner, and I am not the jury, b
there are several matters which have to be brought o
into the open.'

Emma's throat tightened. 'What matters are yo
referring to?'

'I think that first of all we will get Sammy Moodle
out of the way,' he announced, seating himself close
her and stretching his long legs out in front of hi
'Three years ago I had reason to fire him, and sin
then he has been taking his revenge in petty ways whic
have been most annoying. I think it is he wh
frightened you on the beach that night when you we
for a walk.'

'It was him, yes.' She took a steadying sip of win
and the liquid stung all the way down her throat. 'I wa
on the beach one afternoon after that incident, and h
spoke to me. He tried to frighten me away with th
nasty suggestion that there was evil lurking at the vill
and he actually tried to insinuate that—that you
killed your wife. It was Sammy who said that you ha
been seen, but he would not give me the name of h
informant, and when I found Reggie up that tree I p
two and two together, and . . . well, obviously I cam
up with five.'

'Reggie told you the truth.'

She caught her breath in surprise. 'You believe tha

'I have remembered everything now,' he said, lightir
a cheroot while she stared at him in stunned silence.
was on the patio when Marguerite came home that da
and told me that she was going to leave me. I wante
my freedom so badly at that moment that I agreed to
divorce. Suddenly she went wild with anger, th
knowledge that I would give her her freedom no long
seemed to please her, and it is true that she struck o
at me. I caught her wrists in an attempt to calm he
and everything else is as Reggie told you.' His eyes m

hers through a cloud of aromatic smoke. 'I no longer harbour any feelings of guilt on that score, Emma.'

'I'm glad.' Her love for him surged to the fore, but she suppressed it hastily. 'How long have you known the truth?'

'I began to recall a few things that same night after you left me in the study, and every day after that I had visions of certain incidents which you could not have told me about.' He studied the tip of his cheroot briefly, then his eyes met hers. 'She was going away with Louis.'

'I know.' Her fingers tightened nervously about the stem of the glass. 'Louis told me about it the last time we had dinner together.'

A cynical smile touched Julien's mouth. 'It is not like Louis to confess his mistakes.'

'Well, I . . .' She paused and smiled self-consciously. 'I somehow guessed the truth, and I more or less trapped him into a confession.'

Julien's expression sobered. 'You have been very busy lately on my behalf, and I want you to know that I am grateful.'

She wanted his love, but he was offering her gratitude, and she almost cried out with the agony of it. 'Have you spoken to Louis?'

'I have spoken to him, and there are no bad feelings, but he has decided to leave Mauritius and settle in France,' he enlightened her. 'He has an uncle there who has a business he wishes Louis to take over from him.'

'And Sammy?'

'I will do nothing about Sammy,' he set her mind at rest. 'His illicit dealings will one day put him in prison, I am certain of that, and Reggie will no longer have to remain silent about what he saw. I have been to the authorities to settle the matter of Marguerite's death once and for all, and their official finding will be in the newspapers shortly. News spreads fast on this island, and Reggie will be free when he hears of it.'

'I see,' she murmured, staring down into her wine.

The shadow of uncertainty was gone, and the truth had washed away his guilt. The serpent had at last been banished from paradise, but it did not diminish Emma's uneasiness. Everything had been explained, but one matter had been left untouched, and her insides recoiled from the thought. She could not sit there and listen to him telling her calmly that he loved Daniella. That would be asking too much of her.

'Shall I order an early dinner, or would you prefer to eat later?' asked Julien, switching on the reading lamp beside his chair when dusk began to settle in the room.

'I—I'm not very hungry,' she confessed.

'Then we shall eat later,' he agreed.

That strange glitter was back in his eyes and resigning herself to the inevitable, she forced the issue. 'Where is Daniella?'

'Daniella?' He looked somewhat surprised. 'She is enjoying a well-earned holiday in Durban.'

'Oh,' she said, feeling deflated and very bewildered and suddenly nothing seemed to make sense.

Julien raised a quizzical eyebrow. 'Are you not going to ask me where I spent the weekend?'

'It's none of my business, surely,' she protested lowering her lashes to hide the pain and confusion in her eyes.

'It is very much your business,' Julien contradicted quietly. 'When I was in Durban I spent many hours with your charming family.'

'With Lucy and Richard?' she gasped, her hand shaking so much that she had to put down her glass for fear of spilling her wine.

'They are the only family you have, are they not?' he mocked her.

'Yes ... yes, of course,' she stammered foolishly.

'I gave them my personal assurance that you are well, and I also assured them that you shall be well taken care of in the future.'

'Oh,' she said, her bewilderment growing by the second. 'There was no need for you to go to such lengths to set their minds at rest.'

'Your family has every right to know that you will be safe here with me for the rest of your life.'

'For the rest of my life?' Floundering in a sea of confusion, she stared at him, and saw again that strange glitter in his dark eyes. 'What are you talking about?'

'You are an intelligent woman, but tonight you are being very dense, *mon coeur*,' he smiled.

Mon coeur! My heart! He had called her *my heart*. His smile was amused, but the eyes that met hers were grave, and what she saw in their depths made her heart do a mad somersault in her breast.

'Julien, don't——'

'I have the permission of your family to ask you to marry me.'

The world seemed to explode around her. She had wanted this so much that she was quite sure her mind had become warped with longing, and when tears filled her eyes she buried her face in her hands. 'Oh, God, I must be going crazy!' she groaned.

'Emma, please listen to me.' His fingers gently pried her hands away from her face, and she found him kneeling at her feet. 'Will you marry me, Emma, or do you think my unfortunate past will be too much for you to live with?'

'I thought you were going to marry Daniella,' the words spilled from her lips. 'I saw your shadows on the patio beneath my window the night before you left for Durban. I heard you talking, and I saw you kissing her.'

'We embraced,' he corrected sternly. 'And there wa no passion involved. Daniella has been a good frien and she knew that I was going to make my intentio known to your family.'

'Oh, Julien,' Emma sighed weakly.

'Does that mean you will marry me?' he demande his fingers tightening almost anxiously about her wrist

'Oh, yes it does,' she cried, tears sparkling in her ey when she raised them to his, but her heart wa unmistakably there for him to see what he may hav been too blind to see before.

'Mon adorée!' the deep velvet of his voice caressed h and, lifting her bodily out of her chair, he carried h towards the sofa.

They sat with their arms locked about each othe and for long, soul-searching seconds they looked dee into each other's eyes before he lowered his lips to he and kissed her with a tender passion that stirred h more than anything had ever done before. Her hea was beating fast, and it felt as if the blood was singi through her veins when his lips finally left hers to trail path of fire along her throat down to the opening of h blouse.

'Je t'aime, Julien,' she whispered, her voice jer with emotion. 'I love you so very much that I've bee going nearly crazy thinking you could never love me.'

'I think I have loved you from the first time I sa you, but I was sure of it that night on the beach at Bel Mare,' he said against her lips.

'So was I,' she confessed elatedly, and he raised h head to look into her eyes with surprise etching h features.

'You knew it then as well?'

'Yes,' she breathed.

'Emma, *mon coeur.*' His arms tightened about her. ' was not my intention to make you unhappy, but, until knew the truth, I had no right to speak of my feelings for you.'

'I know, and I understand,' she whispered, trailing her fingers in a tender caress along the lean angle of his jaw, and her touch deepened the flame in his eyes.

'You have given me new life, Emma, and I must warn you that, once I have made you mine, I shall never let you go.'

With her heart too full to speak, she pulled his head down to hers, and when their lips met a fire was ignited between them which was not unfamiliar to her, but she had never known it to be so intense. Julien eased her body down on to the sofa with his own, and she knew a sharp, sweet pang of desire when the tiny buttons of her blouse gave way beneath his fingers to allow his hands access to her breasts. His mouth explored the sensitive cord of her throat, and the sensual touch of his fingers on her responsive flesh acquainted her once again with sensations that blotted out everything except the longing to be closer still to his lean, muscled frame above her. His lips teased, excited, and aroused her, and she clung to him, surrendering herself totally to the emotions spiralling through her.

'*Mon Dieu*, Emma, we must make plans,' Julien groaned, drawing away from her slightly, and she gazed up at him with eyes still misty with desire.

'What plans?' she questioned dazedly, sliding exploratory fingers inside the opening of his shirt to caress his hair-roughened chest, but he trapped her wrist between strong fingers to stay her action.

'I am selling the villa,' he said firmly. 'The only reason I have not done so before was because I hoped it would help me regain my memory of what had occurred there, but now there is no longer any reason to continue living in that villa with its unhappy memories.'

'What do you have in mind?' she prompted a little breathlessly.

'I think *Maman* will agree to move back to her home at Roches Noires with Dominic and Nada. Li can stay here in the hotel, and so will we until I have sold the villa and we have found somewhere more suitable.' His warm glance slid over her, and her cheeks felt heated when she realised that the top half of her body was bared for his inspection. 'Do you agree with that?' Julien questioned her.

'Yes, of—of course,' she stammered shyly, attempting to cover herself, but his hand closed over her breast to prevent her, and the pleasure of his touch made her pulse rate soar.

'I will make arrangements for our marriage to take place this Saturday afternoon.'

'This Saturday?' she laughed a little incredulously. 'Isn't that rushing things a bit?'

'I will also make the necessary plans for your family to fly out to attend the ceremony,' he continued somewhat arrogantly, ignoring her protest. 'There will be no honeymoon now, unfortunately, but we can always arrange something later.'

'Oh, Julien,' she sighed tremulously. 'I—I don't quite know what to say.'

His features softened at her obvious confusion. 'Do you agree to marry me this coming Saturday?'

The potent persuasion of his caressing fingers was enough to settle the question in her mind, and her eyes were stormy with emotion when she said huskily, 'I think I have no option but to agree.'

'*Mon adorée,*' he murmured, the deep velvet of his voice vibrant with a mixture of tenderness and desire as he lowered his head to brush his lips against hers. '*Je vous aime.*'

Emma wondered briefly what Madame Celestine

would say. And Dominic? Would it please him to know that she was going to marry his father?

The sensual and demanding pressure of Julien's lips halted her thoughts, and sanity fled for endless minutes while she was given yet another glimpse of the paradise that awaited her as the wife of this forceful, dynamic man. Her logical mind warned that the future may not always be easy. The harm Marguerite had caused might never quite be eradicated, but Emma was determined to bring into their marriage the happiness he had never known before.

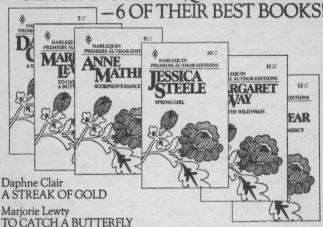